Captain Wentworth Home From the Sea

A Novella

Mary Lydon Simonsen

www.austenvariations.com
Quail Creek Publishing, LLC

Printed in the United States of America
Published by Quail Creek Publishing, LLC
quailcreekpub@hotmail.com
www.marysimonsenfanfiction.blogspot.com

©2011 Quail Creek Publishing LLC
ISBN: 978-061554966-8
ISBN: 0615549667

:

iv

Chapter 1

1814
Kellynch Hall, Somerset

"Retrench?" Sir Walter Elliot, Master of Kellynch, Somerset, said in too loud a voice. "I do not like that word any better than the one you used earlier: *economize*."

"I understand your natural dislike for such terms, Sir Walter," Lady Russell, a family friend and intimate of the baronet's late wife, answered.

Despite the unpleasantness of the topic, the subject of the Elliots' obligations had to be addressed. Knee-deep in debt, Sir Walter was being pressed on all fronts, including an embarrassing confrontation with a merchant in London. Because of that contretemps, even the baronet recognized that something must be done. However, eldest daughter Elizabeth's suggestion that unnecessary charities be cut off and that purchasing new furnishings for the drawing room be delayed did nothing to ease their current financial situation, and so Lady Russell produced a list of economies she had drawn up with the assistance of Anne, Sir Walter's middle daughter, and the only sensible person residing in the house since the death of Lady Elliot more than a dozen years earlier.

"What! Every comfort of life to be knocked off! Journeys, London, servants, horses, table, contractions and restrictions everywhere! To live without the decencies even of a private gentleman! I shall not!" Sir Walter exclaimed after perusing Lady Russell's suggestions. "No, I would sooner quit Kellynch Hall at once than live here on such disgraceful terms." He returned the objectionable document to its owner.

After such a declaration, Lady Russell knew there was nothing to be done except to summon Mr. Shepherd, the Elliots' agent, who was waiting in the wings for the purpose of establishing the conditions for a lease of Kellynch Hall.

In the drawing room, Mr. Shepherd stood before the assembled Elliots. "I must take leave to observe, Sir Walter, that the present juncture is much in our favor. With Napoleon in exile on Elba, this peace will be turning all our rich naval officers ashore, and they will all be wanting a home. Many a noble fortune has been made during the war, and these officers have money to spend. Why should they not spend it here at Kellynch Hall?"

"Supposing I *was* to let the house," Sir Walter said grudgingly, "I have by no means made up my mind as to the privileges to be annexed to it. Of course, the park would be open, but what restrictions I might impose on the use of the pleasure grounds is another thing. I am not fond of the idea of my shrubberies being always approachable, and I should recommend Elizabeth to be on her guard with respect to her flower garden."

Although Anne did not to respond to her father's fit of pique, she lowered her gaze and shook her head in disbelief at his pigheadedness. At Kellynch Hall, they were living in a state of siege, pursued by debt collectors at every turn, and yet her father spoke of the pleasure grounds and garden. If foliage and flowers were higher priorities than paying the family's debts, was it any wonder their finances were in such a state?

"I have other reservations about leasing the estate to a naval officer," Sir Walter continued. "On two points, I find a naval presence offensive. First, it is a means of bringing persons of obscure birth into undue distinction and raising men to honors their fathers and grandfathers never dreamt of. Secondly, it cuts up a man's youth and vigor most horribly. They are all knocked about and exposed to every climate and weather until they are not fit to be seen."

Appearances were of great importance to Sir Walter, none more so than his own and that of his family. He could not pass a mirror without stopping to admire his own countenance, and it distressed him to see that his two younger daughters, both in their twenties, were already fading. Even his dear friend, Lady Russell, had crow's feet, and while the lady continued to babble on about economies, Sir Walter was thinking about sending her a jar of Gowland's lotion to prevent further wrinkling.

"That is an excellent idea, Mr. Shepherd," Anne said, seconding the agent's suggestion. "After all, it is the navy who has done so much for us in keeping Napoleon's forces from our shores, and they should be given at least an equal claim with any other set of men."

Mr. Shepherd jumped at the morsel Anne had served him. "Then I have good news to share. I chanced to encounter Admiral Croft who is looking for a residence in Somerset. As he took so many prize ships during the war, he is a rich man, quite capable of paying the lease on Kellynch Hall. I am confident that he would be willing to pay a premium rate in order to be in his home county."

"But who is this Admiral Croft?" Sir Walter asked. "It is not enough that he is a native of Somerset. My tenants are natives. The butcher, the baker, and the candlestick maker are natives. I need to know more about this Admiral Croft."

"He is a rear admiral of the white," Anne said. "He distinguished himself in the Trafalgar action and has been in the East Indies ever since."

Anne doubted this explanation would make any difference to her father as he had little interest in anything that did not specifically impact his own little world. Napoleon's exile to an island in the Mediterranean, and the reason why so many officers were now on shore, meant nothing to him. Their sacrifice on behalf of their country did not register on any level.

Anne's brief statement was followed by silence, thus allowing Mr. Shepherd to give his reasons why he thought the admiral would make an excellent tenant. "In the first place, Admiral Croft is married to a sensible woman who will see that the manor house is properly cared for. Better yet, there are no children."

Sir Walter acknowledged this bit of information with a nod of approval. The thought of a tribe of little people running through his home with grimy hands, dirty faces, and runny noses revolted him.

"Additionally, Mrs. Croft's brother, Captain Frederick Wentworth, will be with them. Apparently, the captain sustained a serious head wound whilst in the service of his nation that resulted in a loss of memory. It is hoped that his being amongst his family and near to his childhood home in Monkton will aid its restoration."

Hearing the captain's name startled Anne as she had not heard it mentioned for nearly eight years. The mere sound of it brought on a tidal wave of memories, every one of them occurring in 1806, the best year of her life. It was in the year '06 that she had fallen in love with Frederick Wentworth.

After the Battle of Santo Domingo in the West Indies in February of '06, where then Lieutenant Wentworth had distinguished himself, Wentworth had returned to Somerset to reside with his brother Edward, a curate. On a visit to nearby Kellynch Hall, Anne Elliot had been introduced to the young naval officer. Anne, a pretty girl of nineteen, and Frederick, a remarkably fine young man with a great deal of intelligence and spirit, were drawn to each other from the moment of their first meeting. It seemed but a moment before they found themselves deeply in love. It was impossible to say who had been happier: Anne in receiving Frederick's declarations and proposals or Frederick in having them accepted.

A period of unbounded happiness followed, but it was to be short lived. When Frederick applied to Sir Walter for permission to marry his daughter, the young officer's request was answered with a cold stare. As the vain baronet saw no merit in the alliance, or at least nothing that would be of particular benefit to him, Sir Walter stated that he would do nothing for his daughter by way of a dowry. Lady Russell, though more temperate in her criticisms, declared the proposal to be a most unfortunate one as Anne was the daughter of a baronet. And Frederick was... Well, he was a nobody. With both parent and friend working on her young mind, Anne was persuaded to believe the engagement to be hardly capable of success.

Because of Anne's desire to be an obedient daughter, as well as to honor her mother's memory by following the advice of her dearest friend and closest advisor, nineteen-year-old Anne found her resolve to wed Captain Wentworth give way. In the end, she had broken their engagement. In succeeding years, Anne had come to regret her decision, realizing that she would have been happier in maintaining the engagement than she had been in ending it. For eight years, she bore the pain of knowing that when Frederick had left her on that long ago morning, he had taken every chance of her own happiness with him.

When her sister Mary had married their neighbor, Charles Musgrove, brother to Richard, an ensign under the command of Captain Wentworth, Anne had heard news of Frederick by way of Richard's letters to his parents and in correspondence with the family by Captain Wentworth upon the young man's death from a fever. Additionally, Frederick's success on the high seas in seizing many prize ships from the French was duly reported in the newspapers. As a result, Anne knew the captain to be a wealthy man who numbered amongst his acquaintances the Duke of Clarence, an admiral in the Royal Navy and brother to the Prince Regent, as well as members of the aristocracy.

As gratifying as it was to be successful in one's career and to have earned the respect of Britain's elite, Anne wondered if Frederick, because of his injury, was even aware of these excellent connections. What did wealth or prestige matter if the memory of his achievements were denied him?

"Mr. Shepherd, do you know the severity of Captain Wentworth's injury?" Anne asked. "I understand a blow to the head may result in a temporary loss of memory or may cause a person to remember nothing of recent events, and, yet, they may have total recall of events from the distant past. Do you know if either applies to the captain?"

"Miss Anne, I have not met the gentleman, and as such, I cannot answer your question. However, what I do know from Admiral Croft is that the navy insisted Captain Wentworth retire as he was no longer fit to command a frigate."

"Oh, dear!" Anne said, a response ignored by her relations but noted by Lady Russell. Unlike Sir Walter and her sisters, who jettisoned all recollections that did not have them center stage, Lady Russell knew of Anne's love for the captain and of her regrets in not having accepted him. She wondered if the captain's return would be a source of distress for her young friend. In Anne's mind, Lady Russell need not have worried. It was highly likely that Frederick had forgotten about their time together long before his injury had robbed him of his memory.

Chapter 2

Once the plan to quit the ancestral home of the Elliots was finalized, Sir Walter moved with alacrity, and Anne was informed that the family would take up residence in Bath, a city Anne particularly disliked as it was the place where her mother had died. She would have preferred to move to a smaller house in the country, but as she had not been consulted, she had been given no opportunity to voice her opinion. Instead, her assigned role was to see that all the necessary arrangements for the family's move to Bath were made. Additionally, as a representative of the Elliot family, she would visit Kellynch's tenants and the vicar to bid them adieu. As nothing could be done for the merchants by way of repayment, nothing should be said to them until Sir Walter and Elizabeth were safely on the road to Bath. The baronet was unwilling to risk having Kellynch's driveway lined with merchants waving unpaid bills at the passing carriage.

During the morning meal, Sir Walter informed Anne that the Crofts and Captain Wentworth, along with Mr. Shepherd, would arrive at Kellynch for the purpose of signing the lease. "I imagine it will be necessary for some refreshments to be served. See to it, Anne."

Although Elizabeth was the eldest daughter and was greatly enamored of the status afforded by the position of being Miss Elliot, she disliked performing many of the tasks necessary for the proper management of a great house, in particular, meeting with the housekeeper, a woman she referred to as Mrs. Sheets. "All Mrs. Leatherberry cares about is the linen. I have no interest in such things. Anne, *you* must speak with her."

On the other hand, Elizabeth did care about her meals, and she and Cook had become great friends until Mrs. Bridges mentioned the butcher, green grocer, and coalman were all pressing for a discharge of their debts. As Elizabeth thought it unseemly for tradesmen to show up at the servants' entrance begging for payment, and because she was afraid she might encounter such a person, meetings with the cook now fell to Anne as well.

Anne had no objection to the additional duties piled on top of her other responsibilities as she wished to remain busy. In that way, she would have less time to think about the arrival of Captain Wentworth. Every time Anne thought about seeing Frederick after eight years of separation, her body ached, and she could feel a new tear in her heart as an old wound re-opened.

"Perhaps, it is best that Frederick has no memory. In that way, there will be no awkward moments when we are again introduced." In her mind, Anne repeated that statement over and over so that she might come to believe it. "I know it would have been a blessing if *I* had lost *my* memory after Frederick had gone to sea as it would have spared me a great deal of pain." But then Anne shook her head. No, she would *not* have wanted that as her memories of their time together were her sole source of solace since Frederick's departure.

From her first-floor perch, Anne saw the carriage as it pulled into the drive, and after a quick glance in the mirror, she went downstairs. After coming to a halt in front of the portico, she waited for the party to emerge from the conveyance. Admiral Croft, in civilian attire, was the first to step out of the carriage.

"Oh, dear!" Anne said, looking at the well tanned admiral. "Papa will have his stereotype confirmed as he is the color of an orange, and the lines etched in his face are as deep as a furrowed field."

The next to appear was Frederick's sister, Sophia Croft. Although not as weather beaten as her husband, it was obvious she had sailed with the admiral on many occasions. Anne could just imagine the comments her father and Elizabeth would make about Mrs. Croft's lack of attention to her skin, a favorite subject of father and daughter when discussing the people of Somerset. But when one considered that the area was a farming community, what could one expect? Would it even occur to a farmer to spend his hard-earned money on such fripperies as lotions?

Now only Frederick was left. He emerged from the carriage with hat in hand and profile in full view. He was handsomely attired in a blue jacket with gold buttons and tan breeches—clothes very much like what he had worn when she had last seen him. As Captain Wentworth ascended the steps of the portico, Anne's mind drifted back to the scene of their parting. It had been a beautiful morning when Frederick came to Kellynch so full of expectations for a shared life with his betrothed. After receiving him in the parlor, Anne, fighting back tears, informed Frederick that it had been wrong for her to have accepted him without consulting her father and that she must break the engagement. But Frederick refused to surrender to Sir Walter or anyone who worked against him in the pursuit of the woman he loved, and he had asked that she walk with him to the gazebo.

After throwing his hat on a bench, Frederick took Anne in his arms and pleaded with her to come away with him and to disregard the advice of the naysayers who were unaware of the depth of their love. To bolster his case for marriage, he spoke with confidence of a career in the navy, one that would allow him to provide for a wife and family. He also mentioned he had been born lucky and had no doubt his luck would hold.

But to follow Frederick would have required a leap of faith on Anne's part, and without her mother's guiding hand, she was unprepared to do that, and she had stepped away from him. The distress—and anger—she saw in his eyes and the harsh words spoken had broken her heart. By his look, she could see that by not believing in him, she had betrayed him. Without another word spoken between them, Frederick walked to the stables, mounted his horse, and rode south toward the coast without so much as a backward glance. That was the last Anne had seen of him—until today.

The Crofts and Captain Wentworth followed the Elliots' butler to the drawing room where Sir Walter, Elizabeth, the Musgroves, Mr. Shepherd, and Lady Russell awaited them. As their guests approached, Sir Walter whispered to Elizabeth, "I was right. The admiral's face is as orange as the cuffs and capes of our livery."

Elizabeth's response was to snicker at her father's witticism.

"Please allow me to make the introductions," Mr. Shepherd began. After an exchange of bows and curtseys, Lady Russell mumbled a "pleased to make your acquaintance," but other than that lukewarm greeting, the room was as chilly as if the doors had been thrown open on a winter's day. Aware of her role in separating Anne and the captain, Lady Russell looked for clues that Captain Wentworth remembered her and was relieved when she realized he had no recollection of their terse exchange in this very drawing room eight years earlier. Mr. Shepherd's intelligence that the captain had suffered the loss of his memory was accurate.

"Captain Wentworth," Charles Musgrove said, stepping from behind his father-in-law. "My younger brother, Richard, served with you in the East Indies on the *Laconia*. When he died of a fever, you were good enough to write my parents a letter of condolence that proved comforting to them. On behalf of my family, I would like to thank you."

"Mr. Musgrove, I would like to say that I remember your brother, but I received a head injury that has parted me from my memory. All I can say is that I am sorry for your loss, and I am pleased to hear my letter provided some solace for you and your family."

During these exchanges, Anne remained in the foyer, listening to every word spoken by Frederick Wentworth. Realizing that Frederick had no memory of her father or Lady Russell, she understood that it was unlikely he would remember her, either. After taking a deep breath, she entered the drawing room prepared to meet the only man she would ever love.

"Ah, here is Anne, my middle daughter. I forgot all about her," Sir Walter said with a dismissive wave of his hand.

The two men arose and bowed, and Anne tested her supposition that Frederick had forgotten her by looking directly at him. As far as she could tell, there was not a glimmer of recognition on his part, which both relieved and saddened her: relief that there was to be no awkward exchange and sadness because he had forgotten all about her.

The years had been good to the captain. His vigorous occupation demanded that he stay physically fit, and she could see the muscles rippling under his coat, causing her heart to skip a beat. Although his face was tan, it only added to his good looks by accentuating his beautiful blue eyes. Despite some graying at his temples, he was as handsome as the young officer who had kissed her on a beautiful May morning in the spring of her youth.

While tea was being served, Elizabeth, who refused to address the weathered Admiral and Mrs. Croft, asked Captain Wentworth what he thought of Kellynch Hall.

"It is a fine estate," Frederick said, an answer that pleased both father and daughter. "But recently I have been in a great many houses. Other than their libraries, I have little interest in them. Once you have seen one set of French furniture, Persian rugs, and Gobelin tapestries, you have pretty much seen them all. However, your gardens are satisfactory."

Shocked by the abruptness of his comments and fearing his remarks might ruin any plans for leasing the house to the Crofts, Lady Russell suggested that Anne show Captain Wentworth the library.

After Frederick had left the room, Mrs. Croft apologized for her brother's statement. "In addition to his injury robbing him of his memory of names and faces, it seems to have robbed my brother of some of his manners as well. Please understand that Captain Wentworth is a seafaring man, and for the better part of his life, he has lived amongst sailors, a group not given to excessive displays of etiquette."

Charles Musgrove, having found the exchange amusing, came to the captain's defense. "I remember my brother remarking on the salty language of the sailor. When on leave, Richard told many an interesting tale about his voyages and the ports he had visited. Unfortunately, I cannot share them with you as ladies are present," he said, chuckling.

With the tension in the room somewhat dissipated, Mr. Shepherd directed the concerned parties to a desk where the lease was waiting for the signatures of Admiral Croft and Sir Walter. The agent was eager to have the lease signed and sealed before that boorish man emerged from the library causing Sir Walter to rethink leasing the estate to naval officers.

While Anne stood near the door, she watched as Frederick scanned the shelves of Kellynch's library. For the size of the estate, it was not a great library, especially since its most valuable books had been sold to pay the bills, but it was certainly sufficient for a family who, with the exception of Anne, read as little as the Elliots did.

"Your collection tends heavily towards novels and myths," Frederick finally said after taking inventory of the Elliot collection and while thumbing through a copy of Richardson's *Pamela.*

In his declaration, Anne detected a note of censure. "I find novels to be most entertaining."

"No doubt they are adequate for the female mind," Frederick answered, "but I prefer something weightier. When I close a book for the last time, I want to know I have learned something. It is not enough to be merely entertained."

"But there is so much to learn in novels," Anne said, defending her choice of reading.

"Such as?"

"Such as the human condition. When I read Fielding or Richardson, I meet every manner of person in every imaginable situation. I come to know their strengths and weaknesses, their trials and tribulations, their—"

"You *do* know these characters of whom you speak are fictitious?" Frederick asked with a heavy dose of sarcasm.

"Yes, it is true the characters are the author's inventions, but are not their situations representative of scenes of everyday life? As a man of the world, surely you do not limit yourself exclusively to works of non-fiction. What of the ancients, Homer and Virgil, or our own Chaucer and his *Canterbury Tales*? And what is your opinion of Shakespeare? Is there not something to be learned in every one of the Bard's plays? How can you read *Richard III* and not know of palace intrigue or *Henry V* and remain unaware of the horrors of war."

"And *Much Ado About Nothing*? That teaches me what?"

"That we all wear masks to hide our true feelings; decisions made in haste are repented at leisure."

"If you say so," Frederick said, moving to another section of the library.

"If you are looking for Davy's *Researches on Heat and Light* or magazines containing the latest scientific discoveries, you will not find them on our shelves," Anne said exasperated. This man was not her Frederick. With little effort, *her* Frederick could quote lengthy passages from the *Odyssey* and Henry V's St. Crispin's Day speech or wax eloquent while reciting Cowper, Donne, and Pope, but such skills required a memory. Apparently, his injury had resulted in the loss of that part of his education.

"Then there is no reason to remain." The captain stepped to the side so that Anne might pass through the door ahead of him.

* * *

When Anne returned to the drawing room, she found all necessary documents regarding the lease of her home had been signed, and the Crofts were prepared to take possession of Kellynch in ten days' time.

"Hopefully, that will be sufficient time for you to make the necessary arrangements for your move to Bath," Mrs. Croft said, addressing Sir Walter. "If it is not, then we can delay our arrival until it is more convenient for your family, and we shall continue to stay at a hotel in Exeter."

"That will not be necessary," Sir Walter answered, dismissing the generous offer. "Elizabeth and I shall depart in the morning for Bath as we are eager to take up our rooms in Camden Place. I have been informed by a reliable correspondent that people of rank and fashion are already gathering for the winter season, including my cousin, Dowager Viscountess Dalrymple, and her daughter, Miss Carteret," he said, verbally stroking their names. "However, Anne will remain to see that you are properly settled."

"Papa," Anne said with a puzzled look as this was the first she was hearing of such an arrangement, "have you forgotten I am to go with Mary to Uppercross?"

Hearing her name, Mary Musgrove perked up. "Yes, Papa. I must have Anne come home with me. I am unwell and in need of assistance with the boys as Charles is of little help in that regard. With winter coming, there is so much to do, and who, I ask, will do it?"

Sir Walter ignored Mary's protest and turned to his middle daughter. "Allgood and Cook will be coming with Elizabeth and me to Bath, and with Mrs. Leatherberry visiting with her sister in Kent, it is necessary that you be here when Admiral and Mrs. Croft take possession." He then gave her a look to let her know that he believed his tenants capable of carrying off the silver or slipping valuable bric-a-brac out the back door.

"As you wish, Papa," Anne said. Although she had not been consulted, she would make no complaint as her father's dictate delayed her departure for Uppercross and that truly was a relief. Upon arrival at Mary's home, she would be subjected to unending complaints about Charles's lack of interest in his wife, her sons running about the house helter-skelter, the precarious state of her health, and the laziness of the servants. No, this was much better. Smiling, Anne turned her attention to the Crofts and informed them that she would be most pleased to welcome them to Kellynch in a week's time.

After hearing Sir Walter's edict that Anne must remain, Lady Russell gave her young friend a sympathetic look as Anne would be forced to live under the same roof with a man she had once hoped to marry but who now had no memory of her whatsoever.

Chapter 3

Years at sea did things to a man. Shouted orders, constant wind, and the roar of cannon robbed many a naval man of his hearing, and such a thing had happened to Admiral Croft. As a result, he had not heard Frederick's uncomplimentary remark about Kellynch Hall. *Not that he would have cared*, his wife thought, as the nuances of moving in society were lost on the old salt. But Sofia Croft *did* care. For a man of humble origins, rising in society was difficult enough without Frederick providing fodder for people like Sir Walter who looked down their noses at men who had made their mark by virtue of their military service. Although she had not heard the comment made by Sir Walter to his daughter, she had no doubt he was mocking the admiral's appearance. Despite his fine apparel, when a naval man, such as Admiral Croft, walked the streets of London or Bath, he was easily recognized by the coarseness and color of his skin and, very often, by his oaths. Those he encountered would either give way in recognition of his service to his nation or utter unflattering remarks under their breath. It appeared as if Miss Anne Elliot belonged to the first group and her father and older sister to the latter.

Before moving to Kellynch Hall, Sophia wished to discuss the matter of her brother's intemperate comments. In that way, she could head off any unpleasantness that might be occasioned by Frederick speaking the unvarnished truth. Upon their return to Exeter from Somerset, Sophia asked her brother to walk with her in the direction of the cathedral.

"Frederick, I know you have lost much because of your injury. However, it appears that along with your inability to recall faces and names, you have forgotten the basic tenets of civility."

"How have I offended?" Frederick asked genuinely surprised.

Sophia quoted his statement about one great estate looking like all the others. "That is not something that people as puffed up as Sir Walter and Miss Elliot wish to hear."

"Then it is time they were deflated. Except for a fine timepiece in the drawing room, there is nothing in that house to set it apart from a dozen others I have visited in years past. In fact, there are areas in need of improvement. I do not think the manor has seen a coat of paint in a decade, the stables are woefully neglected, and some of the furniture is missing," Frederick said, pointing to impressions in the carpet where the missing pieces once stood.

"You are missing my point entirely."

"No, I am not. It is just that I do not see why we must bow and scrap before the Elliots as if we were serfs on a feudal estate. After all, Sir Walter is only a baronet. From the date in the Baronetage, which, apparently, he regards as highly as his Bible as it is on display in the foyer, his family was awarded—or purchased—the title during the reign of George II, the present king's father—hardly an ancient tie to the monarchy. I remain unimpressed."

Sophia understood a lot of Frederick's inappropriate comments were a result of his frustration with his condition. Although he could speak at length about the house of Viscount Melville, Lord of the Admiralty, he could not supply one detail about the man himself. He spoke enthusiastically of the view of the Chiltern Hills from the home of Lord Grafton, but could neither recall the baron nor any of his children, including one of his sons with whom he had attended the naval academy in Portsmouth. He knew every sail and mast on a frigate, the definition of every naval term, and the miles between ports, but did not recognize his first lieutenant when the man had visited him in hospital at Great Yarmouth.

"For the time being, perhaps it would be best if you said little until you are more comfortable in society," Sophia cautioned her brother.

Frederick knew his sister was right. In the six months since a rogue wave had sent him arse over tea kettle into the wheel of his ship, Wentworth had been struggling. When Sophia and the admiral had first visited him after his injury, it was as if they were strangers to him, but the Crofts had immediately set about to right the ship. While his sister dedicated herself to filling in every detail of his childhood before he had left home for the naval academy, her husband was describing every prize ship he had taken, every port he had visited, every officer making up the crew of the *Laconia*. With great effort, his memory did improve, but before he could be restored to command, it was necessary for *all* of his memory to return.

But Sophia would not give up, and the trio had traveled the breadth of the south of England visiting with shipmates, schoolmates, childhood friends, shopkeepers, his tailor and bootmaker, anyone who might trigger a memory. Although buildings and ships coaxed memories from the recesses of his mind, names and faces continued to elude him.

While recuperating at his brother's parsonage in Shropshire, Wentworth had read every journal he had kept from the time he was old enough to write. The pages of his naval journals revealed the thrill of sailing on his first ship, the pride he felt in being given command of the *Asp*, naval engagements, assuming command of the *Laconia*, privateers taken and accolades bestowed when the frigate had escorted captured ships into Plymouth. There was also the personal. In his private journals, he noted the loss of his parents, his guardian's unsuccessful efforts to secure an apprenticeship aboard one of His Majesty's ships, the loneliness of a lad living away from his brother and sister while attending the naval academy. He wrote of Sophie's joy upon being introduced to Admiral Croft, the marriage of brother Edward and Margaret Tilbury, and the death of Admiral Nelson at Trafalgar and his funeral procession from Greenwich to Westminster Abbey.

While reading the history of his own life, he noted an almost total lack of anything that could possibly be construed as romantic once he had taken command of the *Laconia*. Yes, there was a note here and there about a particularly beautiful or engaging lady with whom he had danced, and one, Adele, with whom he had ridden in a carriage in St. James's Park, but there was nothing to indicate he had ever fallen to their charms.

28

Marriages of friends were noted but with no additional comment. The birth of children earned only a mention of their name and sex. It was as if he begrudged his fellow officers the joy of falling in love and having a family. But if that were the case, then why had he not married? Surely in those eight years, some lady somewhere must have caught his fancy?

After reading his journals and his letters to and from Sophia or having sketches and family portraits thrust in his face, the people who made up his private and public life remained beyond his reach. Finally, the doctors at Great Yarmouth had cut him loose, telling him he might never regain his memory and he must resign his commission. The lone holdout was Dr. Cummings who believed Wentworth might encounter someone from his past who would provide the necessary stimuli so that a full healing could take place. The doctor believed that once the first impediment was dislodged, it would be as if a dam had been removed from a river, and the memories would once again flow freely. Unfortunately, that lone dissenter had not saved him from being forced into early retirement by the navy.

There was one anomaly in all this: Kellynch. Mr. Shepherd had mentioned to Frederick that he had been a visitor to the estate during the summer of 1806. As had been the case with all the other estates he had visited, he fully expected to recognize the manor house once it came into view. However, neither house nor grounds looked familiar to him nor did Kellynch's interior provide a spark. It was as if he had sailed into the doldrums of his memory.

"Frederick! Frederick, are you listening?" Sophia asked.

"Sorry, Sophie. My mind drifted. What were you saying?"

"I was saying that you must try to be more discriminating in your comments."

"Have I insulted anyone other than Sir Walter and Miss Elliot?"

"Not yet. But, remember, Miss Anne Elliot is to remain at Kellynch until the housekeeper returns. Despite her awful family, she seems to be a kind lady. By the way, what did you think of the Elliot daughters?"

"May I speak freely or must I weigh each word as if I were at Carlton Place conversing with the Prince Regent?" Frederick asked with a smile.

"When it is just the two of us, you may speak freely; otherwise, behave yourself," Sophia answered, wagging her finger at him.

With his sister's permission, Frederick proceeded to paint an unflattering portrait of the eldest Elliot daughter. By her looks, it was obvious she held the admiral and his sister in contempt, and by her whispered comments to her father, he knew her to be an unfeeling sort of person. "Although Miss Elliot is the most attractive of the three sisters, her beauty masks an unkind heart."

As for Mary Musgrove, Frederick correctly identified her as a nag and whiner. "When her husband spoke of Richard Musgrove's 'salty language,' she pulled at his sleeve to indicate he should not have said it, and when she learned that Anne would not be returning to Uppercross with her, she pouted like a petulant child."

Sophia could not disagree with either appraisal. "And Anne Elliot?"

"I imagine it is a trial to be the only sensible person in that family."

"Is that all you have to say about the lady?"

"I suspect she was once a beauty, but now has a somewhat haggard appearance. It would help if she did something with her hair—some curling about the face. On such a short acquaintance, all I can say is she appears to be a woman of sense. When we spoke in the library, I challenged some of her notions about what constitutes good reading material, and she came back at me with somewhat persuasive arguments. Although I have no intention of reading novels, she did make a case for others doing so."

"So, you liked her?" Sophia asked.

"Yes, I did. But whether I liked her because she contrasted with her family, whom I did not like, is yet to be known."

"All I ask is that you be polite to Miss Anne during our time together at Kellynch Hall. In my opinion, it will make a nice change from how her family treats her. They order her about as if she were a servant."

"I shall be on my best behavior."

Despite the promise of good behavior, Sophia wondered if his best behavior would be good enough.

* * *

Anne lay on her bed staring at the pleated yellow silk of her canopy. Buying the fabric was the last outing mother and daughter had shared together. While in London, they had visited the draper, and Lady Elliot and thirteen-year-old Anne had settled on the lovely fabric, the color of sunrise, for her bed covers and curtains. Shortly after the curtains were hung, her dear Mama had taken ill. A journey to Bath had failed to provide a cure, and she had passed away in that damp town with rain playing tattoos on the windows. Although fourteen years had passed, in Anne's heart, it was just a moment in time as she felt her mother's presence in nearly every room of the house—the house her father had just taken away from her—and a bitterness swelled up in her breast.

How cruel life was, Anne thought, to be deprived of a devoted parent who loved her, only to be reared by a father who cared not a whit about her. No, that was not true. He *did* care about her ability to manage a house, supervise servants, nurse those who were ill, and placate disgruntled merchants. As for her own personal happiness, she was on her own. If only she had recognized his selfishness before she had agreed to break her engagement to Frederick, how different her life would have been.

Anne turned on her side and her thoughts turned to Frederick Wentworth. *Frederick! Yes, Frederick!* She delighted in saying his name and said it again and again. And his baritone! How musical it sounded! And when he walked into the drawing room, how she had admired his well-shaped calves and broad shoulders and the confidence of his gate. But there was also the terrible scar on his forehead, a reminder of the seriousness of the injury that had cost him his memory—but not his wit. While his remark about Kellynch being like every other great house was met with a stony silence by Elizabeth and Papa, it had greatly amused her. It was a rare event to see the pair of them cut down a size or two, and she sensed that Frederick knew his remark had taken the wind out of their sails. *Well done, Frederick!*

But then there had been their unfortunate time together in the library. Not only did he disapprove of her choice of reading material, but he implied that only a weak mind read such drivel. Such intolerance was not reminiscent of the Frederick she knew and loved. No, not loved, in the past tense, but loves, as in the present. From the moment she had seen him on the drive, she knew her love for him still burned brightly.

Being of a practical nature, Anne understood the next week or so would be her last chance to be in Frederick's company as she must go to Uppercross and then Bath, but it was her intention to savor their time together. Was it within the realm of the possible that they might walk about the pleasure gardens or traverse a country lane? She hoped so. Even a hint of their former time together would cause her soul to sing. And although the pain associated with their earlier parting would return once she departed Kellynch, it was a pain she was willing to bear.

Chapter 4

"Why did Miss Anne not speak at supper?" Frederick asked his sister after their first meal in the dining room of Kellynch Hall.

"I am sure she feels awkward," Sophia answered. "Although Kellynch is her home, she is no longer mistress of the house. Because we pay the lease, she defers to us."

"I agree it is awkward, but not just for her. Having someone sit across the table from you and merely nod or smile is truly disconcerting. I know Miss Anne to be intelligent woman," Frederick said, thinking of her reference to Davy's *Research on Heat and Light*. "I would prefer it if she would join in the conversation. Deference does not equate to silence."

"Then you should address your questions directly to her," Sofia said. "It is not like you to stand on ceremony."

"Very well. I shall."

The next evening, Frederick put his words into action, but his questions were more on the order of an interrogation than a conversation: "Miss Anne, when you were in school in Bath, what did you study? Do you speak any foreign languages? Have you ever visited the Continent? Do you go to London for the Season? Whilst in Town, what draws your interest?" and on and on through most of the evening.

After Anne had retired, Sofia cautioned her brother that he should not view a discussion with a lady as something akin to taking a prize ship. A more delicate approach would serve him better. But as a captain used to barking commands, it was easier said than done, and progress on that front was measured in inches.

"Miss Anne, do you have a decent horse in your stables so that I might ride in the morning?" the captain had asked during their mid-day meal.

Anne, who had grown accustomed to the new Frederick, chuckled at his bluntness. "Yes, but only one that would suit you." Because most of the horses had been sold to pay the carriage maker, blacksmith, farrier, wainwright, and saddler, among others, only the noble Galahad, a handsome roan, remained that would answer for a man of the captain's height and weight. "His name is Galahad, and although a little long in the tooth, he is an admirable animal."

"Did someone say admiral?" Admiral Croft asked, his sojourn in the country having done nothing to improve his hearing.

"No, dear," Mrs. Croft said, placing her hand on her husband's arm. "Miss Anne said *admirable* not *admiral*." Turning to Frederick, she suggested her brother walk to the stables and have a look at Galahad for himself. "Perhaps Miss Anne will accompany you."

As they walked, Frederick asked his companion if she rode.

"I have not ridden in years."

"That is not what I asked you," Frederick bluntly answered. When Anne did not respond, he softened his tone. "Why do you not ride?" But then he provided the answer to his question. "It is because you have the duties of the mistress of the manor, and your leisure time is limited."

"Yes, that certainly is part of it, but not all. The fact is I have never enjoyed riding alone. Other than Mary, there is little enthusiasm for it in my family, and Mary has not ridden since the birth of her first child."

"Motherhood should not prevent a lady from riding. Lady Grafton is the mother of a brood of six, and she rides every day."

"I am all admiration for Lady Grafton; however, Mary is often unwell."

So, in addition to being a chronic whiner, she pretends to be an invalid, the captain thought. "When I was in her company, she looked as fit as fiddle to me."

"Her illnesses come and go," Anne said, trying to hide her smile. Although she knew Mary's ailments were merely a ploy to gain the attention of her husband and his family, Anne continued to visit Uppercross because she enjoyed the company of her brother-in-law, delighted in the antics of her nephews, and welcomed visits with Mr. and Mrs. Musgrove and their daughters, Louisa and Henrietta.

"Her illnesses come and go, do they? Do they *come* so you will *go* to Uppercross?"

"Captain, that is unkind." With Sophia's caution in his ear, Frederick looked properly chastened, but then Anne absolved him of his sin with a smile. "It is Mary's way of gaining Charles's attention."

"I believe such a ploy is a weapon in the arsenal of many ladies. Since my injury, I have been a guest in many a drawing room and have observed such things. It seems many wives suffer from various ailments that just happen to coincide with the shooting or hunting season."

"Charles would rather shoot than do anything else, that is, except to buy a gun to go shooting with," Anne said, acknowledging the truth of Frederick's statement.

"Will you admit your sister's ailments are in her head?"

"Captain, you are too severe upon my sex. You mention a female arsenal, but in truth, our weapons are few, and we use what is available. Of necessity, ladies must employ arts and allurements to gain the attention of our male counterparts. It is certainly not unique to Mary."

"Yes, I have noticed, but, personally, I have little patience for such games. At a ball, I watched a lady dropped her fan three times so that different gentlemen might recover it. It got to the point where I was prepared to tie it to her wrist."

"Were her efforts successful in gaining the gentlemen's attention?"

"Yes."

"Then her ploy worked. Possibly, it would be less objectionable to you if you thought of such actions in nautical terms. The lady in question had set her eyes on three prize ships, that is, those three particular gentlemen. Dropping her fan allowed her to observe them at close quarters, and when the time was right, she launched an attack on one of them. In doing so, she captured the ship."

To Anne's surprise, Frederick burst out laughing. "You have succeeded in showing me the error of my ways. Instead of despising the lady, I now find I admire her."

As they neared the stables, the captain suddenly stopped and asked Anne if they had ever met before.

"Why do you ask such a question?" she said, her heart nearly jumping out of her chest.

"Because Mr. Shepherd says we did meet—that I was a guest at Kellynch several years ago."

"Yes, we have met," Anne answered, relieved that the memory of their romance had not returned. "You were staying with your brother when he was still at Monkton and occasionally came to Kellynch to dine or to use our stables."

"Did you and I talk?"

"Yes, on several occasions, we did."

"And what did we speak of?"

"Nothing of note," Anne answered after a long pause. "Certainly not the weighty matters you spoke of in the library. Our conversations were all light and air."

For a fleeting moment, Anne was tempted to tell Frederick that when they were together they spoke of anything and everything. While he would go on at length about his aspirations to be the best officer in His Majesty's Navy, she spoke of what adventures she would experience as the wife of an officer while visiting faraway stations: tasting exotic foods, observing the natives of distant lands, and viewing unfamiliar landscapes. They spoke of books, the theater, politics, and the changing map of Europe, as well as a home near the sea. But mostly they talked about their future and the children they would have.

"In other words, drawing-room babble," Frederick said in a dismissive tone.

"Yes, nothing but babble. And here we are at the stables. I shall introduce you to Mr. Ferris and return to the house."

"Must you go?" In their weeks together, Frederick had found he craved her company like no other. There was a calmness about her that made him feel at ease. When in her presence, his mind was less muddled and snippets of his personal history were returning. "I know you have responsibilities at the manor house, but do they include clearing the table and washing the dishes, Miss Anne Elliot?"

"No, they do not, Captain Wentworth, but the person responsible for preparing all your meals is in need of direction. Until my father departed with our cook, Alice was merely the cook's assistant. Therefore, I must go to her. But I leave you in the capable hands of Mr. Ferris. Good evening, Captain."

But Anne had not seen the last of Frederick. When the captain returned from the stables, he went looking for her and found her in Mr. Allgood's office leaning into the light of a candle while making entries in the household accounts ledger. He could tell by her sagging shoulders that there was more red ink than black to be entered.

"I have spoken to Mr. Ferris, and I am to ride tomorrow," Frederick told her. "During our conversation, he informed me that you are an excellent rider, so I am asking if you will take some time from supervising the cook and keeping the household accounts to ride with me? You and I are of a similar mind in this matter. I prefer not to ride alone."

"Did Mr. Ferris not tell you that except for an occasional ride into the village, I have not ridden in four years?"

"Then you are overdue, aren't you?"

* * *

The next morning, the two riders emerged from the stables when the dew was still on the grass and the sun barely skirting the treetops.

"Miss Anne, I would ask that you take the lead. After all, you know where the best views are."

"Very well, I shall," she said, spurring her dappled gray onward. "There is an excellent view on a nearby hill that looks down on the Winthrop estate. Its owner, Charles Hayter, has recently taken orders and is expected to marry Charles Musgrove's younger sister, Henrietta."

"Really? Miss Henrietta intends to marry a curate?"

"Yes, why?"

"When I dined at Uppercross Abbey, I met the young lady. Although I found Miss Henrietta to be quite pleasant, she is given to fits of giggling. It is my understanding that curates' wives are absolutely forbidden to so much as titter, no less giggle, and they are absolutely forbidden from laughing out loud. At least that is the case with the wife of my brother, a curate in Shropshire."

"Captain, you are terrible," Anne said, reprimanding him for his statement. "There is no law

43

forbidding the wife of a curate from laughing, and I am sure your sister-in-law has a sense of humor."

"You would not say that if you had met her."

"Perhaps, she is intimidated by your over-powering presence."

Frederick admitted that that was a possibility. "Whenever I visit the parsonage, Margaret makes herself scarce which is no small feat in such a small dwelling. Apparently, my propensity to speak what I find unsettles her."

"So what you are really saying is that Henrietta Musgrove giggles excessively when compared to your sister-in-law. When you look at it in that light, it does make a difference."

"I concede the point," Frederick said, nodding at Anne's logic.

"Did you meet Henrietta's sister, Louisa?"

"Yes, after supper, Charles asked that I accompany him to a neighbor's house for the purpose of looking at a gun he is keen to own before pheasant season begins. When we returned to Uppercross, we found both ladies visiting with your sister, Mary. Miss Musgrove is a fine looking woman, but rather clumsy. While I was there, she tripped over her own feet and nearly fell down the stairs. Fortunately, I was there to cushion her fall. Bruised or not, she will make someone a handsome wife."

"Yes. Yes, she will," Anne stuttered at the mention of the word *wife*. "We are to turn here. You can just make out Winthrop in the distance."

Fortunately, for Anne, the path narrowed, preventing any further conversation about Louisa Musgrove. There was no avoiding the fact that Louisa was a lovely young lady with an agreeable disposition. Considering Kellynch's proximity to Uppercross, there was little doubt many opportunities would arise for the captain to be in Louisa's company. Being nineteen years of age, attractive, and well dowered, she would make Frederick the perfect wife.

After declaring the view to be excellent, Frederick returned the discussion to Louisa. "Miss Musgrove was enthralled with the idea that my sister had crossed the Atlantic four times with Admiral Croft. She declared that if she loved a man she would always be with him. She dismissed the dangers of being on the high seas and made the remarkable statement that she would rather be overturned by her husband than driven safely by anybody else. What do you think about that, Miss Anne?"

"Before I give you my opinion, I shall hear yours as I have heard that many officers are superstitious about women being aboard ship for any reason." Anne knew her response was a dodge, but she needed time to think as she found the captain's interest in Louisa unsettling.

"I think it a bad idea as it is impossible for a woman to be made comfortable when a ship is out on the open sea. Although I do not remember faces and names, my recollections of life on board ship remain intact, and it is not something I would wish for a lady. The accommodations are cramped, and there are many days when even the most seasoned sailor suffers from seasickness. Even the gallant Nelson suffered from bouts of *mal de mer*. I have done so myself on more occasions than I would care to admit. However, when I stated my opinion on the subject to my sister, she chastised me severely. She declared women to be rational creatures who do not expect to be in smooth water all of their days."

"If you think it is a bad idea, Captain, then you will be disappointed in my response as I agree with your sister. In my opinion, if the wife of the captain is willing to suffer the inconvenience of life on board ship, then why should she not be with her husband? Lengthy separations can be the death of a marriage."

"But if love is true and deep, then nothing but the passing of one's spouse can cause love to die."

"You speak of the death of love as if it only occurs as a result of the actions of the couple themselves. Love can perish because of blows rendered by forces beyond their control."

"Such as?"

"A family objecting to the marriage."

"Are you saying a woman would allow all embers of love to die because of family opposition?"

"No, on the contrary, I do not think the embers would go out for the lady as women do not forget men as soon as men forget us."

"I disagree with your supposition," Frederick said emphatically, but he wasn't sure why. As far as he knew, he had never been in love.

"You may disagree, but I assure you that, in this, you are wrong. Women live at home, quiet, confined, while men have a profession or pursuits of some sort to take you back into the world. Continual occupation and change soon weaken impressions. All the privilege I claim for my own sex is that of loving longest when all hope is gone."

"No, I will not allow it to be more a man's nature than woman's to be inconstant and forget those they love. I believe the reverse. Because our bodies are stronger, so are our feelings."

"Captain, you speak eloquently for your sex, and I hope I have done the same for mine," Anne said in a tone indicating this conversation had come to an end. Without his memory to guide him, Frederick was limited to spouting hypotheses while Anne could draw on the real experience of having loved him for so long without so much as a glimmer of hope to sustain her.

As the pair rode back to Kellynch, Frederick wondered if Miss Anne was speaking from personal experience. If that were the case, it would be unfortunate as she was a kind lady worthy of the love of a good man.

Chapter 5

With Kellynch Hall free of the most annoying Elliots, for the first time since her mother's death, Anne was enjoying the public rooms. No longer relegated to her bedchamber or the library, she walked the halls, looking into the various rooms as if she were the visitor and not Frederick and the Crofts.

Anne was relishing her new-found freedom so much that she had written to Mrs. Leatherberry to say that, if she wished, the housekeeper should extend her visit with her sister and was pleased when Mrs. Leatherberry responded she would do just that. Without a housekeeper, Anne informed Mary after Sunday services that she had no idea when she would be available to come to Uppercross for a visit.

"Nonsense, Anne," Mary protested. "Mrs. Croft has sailed the seven seas with her husband without benefit of a housekeeper; therefore, I do not see why you must wait for Mrs. Leatherberry to return to Kellynch before coming to Uppercross. The Crofts do not need you, but I do! My health is indifferent, and with the children running willy-nilly about the house, my nerves are in shreds."

"What about Charles?"

"You cannot be serious. You know very well that Charles is of no assistance in that regard. He endlessly indulges little Charles and Walter, giving into their every whim. They listen to no one but you. I need you by my side, Anne. You *must* come."

For the first time in her life, Anne thought only of herself and refused to budge. She would not leave the company of a man who had once told her she had captured his heart and that it belonged to her alone and for all time. Even though she understood those words belonged to the past, she could still pretend they had a future together because her imagination was all that was left to her. And there was nothing that could more quickly destroy the illusion of romance than a visit to Uppercross with Mary, or so she thought.

* * *

With her brother's impaired memory never far from her mind, Sophia Croft believed its cure could be found in discussions of the navy. As Richard Musgrove had served as an ensign under Frederick, Sophia had hinted to the elder Musgroves that an invitation to dine at Uppercross Abbey would be greatly appreciated, and Mrs. Musgrove, with two unmarried daughters and a son's memory to preserve, was happy to oblige.

During dinner, Sophia directed the conversation in such a way that all topics had a decided naval bent. The mere mention of the *Asp* had Louisa bolting out of her chair in search of the navy lists so that she might read about the first ship the captain had commanded.

"You will not find the *Asp* in those listings, Miss Musgrove," Captain Wentworth told her. "I was the last man to command her. She has since been broken up, or so I have been told."

"So you remember something of the *Asp*, do you?" Admiral Croft asked. "I say that for an old built sloop, you would not see her equal. You were a lucky fellow to get her. Lucky fellow to get anything so soon and at such an age."

"I felt my luck, Admiral, I assure you. I remember being well satisfied with my appointment."

"Do you remember anything else, Frederick?" Sophia eagerly asked.

"Yes. I remember the *Asp* did all that was expected of her. I knew we should either go to the bottom together, or she would be the making of me. In my passage home from the East Indies, I had the good fortune to fall in with the very French frigate I had wanted to take, and I brought her into Plymouth harbor to the cheers of those gathered on shore. How fast I made money in her," Frederick said with a sigh. "I was sorry to hear she was broken up for salvage."

"What year was that, Captain Wentworth?" Louisa asked.

"1806. It was a great object with me, at that time, to be at sea."

"Why was that?"

"I do not know," Frederick said, shaking his head. "All I can remember is that I was eager to be off. I wanted to be doing something."

"Perhaps, you had broken some poor girl's heart and needed to get away," Charles Musgrove teased.

"More likely the lady broke mine," Wentworth answered, laughing. "But why do we speak of broken hearts? We should be dancing." Turning to Anne, he asked, "Miss Anne will you oblige us with a tune on the spinet? I am told you are an accomplished musician." After Anne had given her consent, the others assisted in pushing the furniture to the perimeter so they might dance.

For most of the evening, Anne played while others danced. At one point, she heard Frederick ask the Musgrove sisters why Miss Anne did not engage in such lively entertainment. Henrietta and Louisa were quick to assure him that "she has quite given it up." But that was not completely true. Anne *would* have danced—if only Frederick had asked.

Chapter 6

As autumn waned, the residents of the manor house wanted to make the most of the good weather before the arrival of winter and spent many hours walking the grounds of Kellynch. Sir Walter would have been distressed if he had seen his tenants' daily use of the gardens, but with vibrant colors from an array of late autumn flowers poking out of every corner, the call to be out of doors was too strong to be resisted. Each morning, Frederick stopped by the small office where the account ledgers for the house were stored for the purpose of convincing Anne to leave her work so they might walk in the park or, better yet, go riding.

Anne usually gave in to the captain's requests, but today it was necessary for her to decline. "Thank you, Captain Wentworth, but I cannot ride today. I have fallen behind in my correspondence, and I have dedicated the day to that pursuit."

"May I ask who your correspondent is that he or she would deny you a ride on such a beautiful day?"

"Because you ask, I shall tell you," Anne answered while returning her pen to the inkwell. "I am responding to a letter from an auction house in London. We are very near to an agreement on selling some of the furniture."

This statement did not come as a surprise to the captain. While in the village, Wentworth had seen Anne going into the various shops. When she reappeared empty-handed and with head bowed, he understood her purpose had been to negotiate a delay of payment with the shopkeepers. And now it had come down to selling off the contents of the manor house.

"Is it possible that one night I shall go to my bedchamber and find my bed gone?" Frederick asked in an attempt to lighten her mood. He could see such an admission was an embarrassment to her.

"Of course not, Captain. I would definitely see that you had a cot."

"Being a navy man, I would insist on a hammock."

"Then you must supply your own as you will not find a hammock so far inland." Anne smiled in gratitude at Frederick's attempt to make light of such a grave matter.

"In all seriousness, may I inquire as to the pieces under consideration?"

"You have not seen these particular furnishings. They belonged to my mother and have been stored in the attic since..." But then Anne stopped.

"Allow me to finish your sentence, '...since the arrival of those wretched naval officers.' Oh, do not be embarrassed. I am well aware of the feelings of your family. It was rather obvious that your father would have preferred a tenant who was, shall we say, less brown."

"You heard his comment then? I had hoped you had not."

"Yes, but there was no sting in it as I have heard it many times before. Now, if such a remark had been uttered by Miss Anne Elliot, then I *would have* been hurt. But you are very different from your father and sisters. Thank goodness."

"Captain, please. You are speaking of my family."

"Diplomacy is not my strong suit. I always speak the truth. But as to the matter of your mother's furniture, may I suggest you first speak with Sophia. She may wish to buy the pieces, and as long as she is here at Kellynch, you will be able to enjoy your mother's furnishings."

Anne was touched by the captain's kindness in making such an offer, but she advised him that the negotiations with the auction house were too far along. "There can be no delay as we are seriously in arrears with the grocer and other merchants, and the servants' wages are due, so there is no help for it. The auctioneer has agreed to advance a sum sufficient to meet our immediate obligations; therefore, I must act now. Besides, my mother would want me to do the right thing."

"Would you consider a loan from me?"

"No, Captain, I would not," Anne said emphatically. "I am grateful for your offer, but it would merely delay the inevitable. The wolf is at the door, and I must deal with him now."

Although Frederick had failed in his efforts to have Anne ride with him on this particular day, his attention to their hostess had not gone unnoticed by his sister.

"Frederick, you and Anne have been spending a lot of time together," Sophia said as she worked on her needlepoint in front of a fire and near the chair of her sleeping husband.

"And who would I spend my time with if not her?"

"Charles Musgrove is nearby."

"And so is his wife."

Sophia rolled her eyes at her brother's comment. Although improvements had been made in the matter of polite discourse, Frederick's comments still had an edge to them, and he was quite capable of uttering unkind remarks with little understanding of their impact, such as the one he had just made about Mary Musgrove.

"I think you like Anne very much."

"I *do* like her, so much so that I am thinking of making her an offer," Frederick responded as if this was nothing out of the ordinary.

"What! What are you saying, Frederick?" Sofia said, putting down her needlework. "Have you fallen in love with Anne?"

"No," Frederick answered truthfully. "But I have been in society enough to know I have no wish to subject myself to all that is required to secure the affections of a young lady such as Louisa Musgrove. I do not want to go to balls or breakfasts or for carriage rides in the park. Nor do I want to pay endless compliments about fine fingering and painted tables. Besides, Anne possesses those characteristics I would want in a wife: maturity, honesty, and frankness. Additionally, she has demonstrated that she is capable of managing a household. She is firm, but fair, with the servants and generous to those who need her attention. As for her beauty, she is handsome enough to satisfy."

"You sound as if you are writing an advertisement for a wife. How very unromantic of you."

Frederick merely grunted.

"But I do see that your opinion of Anne's physical charms have changed from 'haggard' to 'handsome enough to satisfy.'"

"Yes, my opinion *has* changed. Perhaps it is our long walks in the gardens that have restored the glow of youth. I do not know. I prefer not to dwell on such things. But as for being romantic, are you implying there was a time when I *was* romantic?"

"Yes, there was a time when you were *very* romantic and spoke of your desire to find someone who would 'pierce your soul'—a soul mate who would walk beside you all the days of your life."

"Those were my words: 'pierce my soul?'"

Sophia nodded.

"Such words could only have been spoken by a man who was deeply in love."

"Yes, you were in love, but everything I know about the lady was contained in one letter sent to me in the summer of 1806 from Monkton. In your missive, you wrote eloquently of a young woman with chestnut hair, blue eyes, and a smile that could light up a room. After declaring your love for this enchanting creature, you indicated that you soon hoped to call her wife. But in your very next letter, you wrote of rejection and heartache, giving no details as to the cause of your separation."

"What was her name?" Frederick asked, leaning forward in his chair to hear his sister's answer.

"I am sorry, Frederick. You never mentioned her name, referring to her only as 'my darling.'"

Frederick went silent. With the clock ticking away the minutes, Sophia studied her brother. Sitting by the fire with the flames casting shadows on his face, she could see the wheels spinning and wondered if her words had sparked a glimpse into his past and asked him if that were the case.

"I do not know," Frederick answered, and he started to pace. "Since coming to Kellynch, I have been having these dreams where I come upon a lady standing in a meadow with her back to me. Even though she does not look at me, she is aware of my presence and waves me on, but when I reach the spot where she was standing, she is gone. And then I wake up."

"Were you not able to make her out at all? Perhaps she is the chestnut-haired beauty of whom you wrote."

"Other than that she had dark hair, no, there were no physical characteristics to define her." Frederick returned to his chair, sinking back into its thick cushion. "Sophie, this chestnut-haired beauty of whom we speak could walk into this room, and I would not recognize her, so why should I not marry someone as agreeable as Anne Elliot and start anew, especially since Miss Anne has no prospects?"

"Why do you say that she has no prospects?"

"When I called on Charles Musgrove at Uppercross, he asked me how everything was going here at Kellynch, and I said very well. He attributed our pleasant stay to Miss Anne's competence and mentioned that he had once asked the lady to marry him."

"But she refused him?" Sophia asked in a surprised voice. "I wonder why?"

"Apparently, the offer was declined without explanation, but Musgrove suspected the reason was that she had lost her heart to another. He speculated that it must have been a very brief affair because he knew nothing of the fellow, and Mary had never mentioned him. With so few eligible gentlemen in the neighborhood, Charles wondered if Anne had come to regret her refusal of his proposal because it was unlikely she would have another."

"From that remark, it sounds as if Charles Musgrove is the one who suffers from remorse because of his subsequent offer to Anne's sister."

"Sophie, I was being charitable in not mentioning Mary Musgrove. You see, I am following your advice and am trying to be less critical of my neighbors."

"How admirable."

"Thank you."

"You misunderstand me. I was referring not to you but to Anne. Despite her dreadful family, she refused an offer from a man of steady character and someone who would have set her up in a fine home very near to Kellynch. Why would she do such a thing?" After a moment's consideration, Sophia added, "To my mind, there is only one answer: She must have loved another, or she would never have refused Charles Musgrove."

Sophia went quiet for several minutes. In their weeks together, she had developed a deep affection for Anne Elliot. In addition to making the new residents of Kellynch welcome in her home, she had demonstrated core values of honesty, kindness, and integrity. She would make a wonderful wife for any man. Why should she not marry Frederick?

"Well, I daresay with such a family and the financial straits the Elliots find themselves in that she will accept you," Sophia said while looking at the worn fabric on the arms of the chair—another indicator of the decline of the Elliots of Kellynch Hall. "But, my dear brother, please allow me to caution you. As a young man you were adamant that you would marry only for love, not convenience or position."

"I have memory enough to know that life makes hash of such notions," Frederick said with a snide laugh. "According to you, I have already experienced the heights of love, only to find my dreams with this mystery lady dashed—and according to your recollection, quickly done. Although I do not love Anne Elliot, I like her very much. The only question remaining is where would we live? I have no home."

"Why you would live here with the admiral and me."

"I have no wish to intrude any more than I already have."

"You would be doing me a favor," Sophia said, looking at her sleeping husband. "Poor Edgar! Ever since he was put on shore, he has lost his way. He honestly doesn't know what to do with himself, and so he sleeps. I never thought I would say this, but I wish the war had not come to an end."

"You are not the only one saying it. When you were dragging me about the country in hopes of restoring my memory, many of my fellow officers were voicing the same complaint. But, at present, I am not fit for command. So, for the time being, I must content myself with being a country squire."

"But until you find your own place, please do make Kellynch your home and Anne's as well, that is, if she accepts you. But I cannot think of any reason why she would refuse you."

"There is one possible impediment. If this man that Anne loved so deeply still lives, then she may very well refuse me."

"That is a possibility, but I think an unlikely one. You are not the only one I have been watching. I have observed Anne as well. She likes you very much."

"I cannot think why," Frederick said, laughing. "She has taken me to task on several occasions for my outspoken remarks, but if Anne accepts me, she will know exactly what she is getting by way of a husband. I have worn no mask nor made any false statements in an effort to win her hand. In all things, I have spoken honestly."

"I can certainly attest to the truth of that statement," Sophia acknowledged.

After looking down at her needlework, she smiled. In addition to her brother's happiness, Sophia was eager to see Anne freed from the shackles that bound her to her ungrateful family. Besides, a marriage would benefit both of them: Frederick needed a wife, and Anne needed a protector. In Sophia's mind, a union of the two was an excellent outcome. And then Sophia chuckled. Although Admiral Croft was less than thrilled with life in the country, leasing Kellynch had proved to be beneficial to at least two people.

Chapter 7

"Excuse me," Anne said, staring at Frederick as if he were a freak in a traveling show. There had been no prelude to the speech he had just delivered. To the contrary. During their morning ride along the bridle path that bisected Kellynch's parkland, little, if anything, had been said. They had grown so comfortable in each other's company that it was possible to remain silent while enjoying a sun-soaked autumn day. But once in the stables, Frederick had asked Anne if she would walk with him to the gazebo. Her first inclination had been to say no because of its sad history as the place of their parting. But Frederick had no recollection of the terrible scene that had taken place there, and so she had agreed. However, she would never have guessed the reason for his request.

"I said, 'Will you marry me?'"

"I do not understand."

"What don't you understand, Anne? Marriage is a union between a man and a woman for the purpose of having children." When Anne said nothing, Frederick elaborated. "You walk down the aisle, stand before the parson, he pronounces you man and wife, you sign the register—"

"I know what marriage is, but why me?" a bewildered Anne asked.

"Because I like you. You are a kind person, and I fully expect you will make a good wife and mother to my children."

"Surely you wish to marry for love, and I know you do not love me."

"I am surprised that a person of your situation in life should find the idea of two people coming together who are not in love to be so unconventional. It is my understanding it was once expected that your sister Elizabeth should marry her cousin, Mr. William Elliot, whom she barely knew, and Charles Musgrove asked your sister to be his wife only after being turned down by you."

Anne blushed at Frederick's reference to Charles's proposal. In the intervening years, she had thought little of it because she had rejected him without giving it a moment's consideration. The very idea of going to the marriage bed with a man she did not love was repellant. But, in the end, even that didn't matter. She knew she would never marry anyone other than Frederick Wentworth. And here he was asking her to be his wife.

"Do I need to court you, Anne? Shall I tell you that you are pretty or speak of your beautiful blue eyes? Shall I mention that I admire your intelligence, your wit, your charm? Or should we discuss more practical matters, such as my fortune and the marriage settlement?"

"I do not need to hear false praise," Anne said, "nor is it necessary for you to itemize your assets or the distribution of them. My concern is simpler. Do you honestly believe I can make you happy?"

"Again, I am surprised by your question. You should be asking if *I* can make *you* happy, and I believe the answer to both questions is yes. I have had the pleasure of your company for two months now, and in that time, I have found you to be most agreeable. Can you say the same about me? I see that you are too polite to reply, so I shall answer for you. I do not know what I was like before I lost my memory, but I cannot imagine that my injury altered me to such an extent that I am no longer the person I was before I collided with a ship's wheel. I am convinced my core being is the same. I have put on no airs for you. I am as you see."

Anne was speechless. She could merely shake her head in confusion.

"Your question to me should be: what it is that *I* shall bring to the marriage."

"Very well. What will *you* bring to the marriage?"

"In addition to being intelligent and a fine specimen of a man," Frederick said, grinning while showing her his profile, "I have been told my finest quality is my sense of loyalty. If you were to consent to be my wife, I would be a devoted husband and father. I might not whisper sweet nothings in your ear, but I will take care of you and any children we may have. Finances will no longer be a concern, and from what I know of your family, that is no small matter. You deserve better, and from me, you will have it."

With her mind in turmoil, Anne walked away from him and stared out at the expansive lawn surrounding the gazebo. Should she just thank Providence for such a gift and accept Frederick or should she confess that this was not the first time he had made such an offer? After a moment's thought, she knew she could not tell him of their past. Her earlier rejection of his proposal might anger him, causing him to withdraw his offer. Her heart could not take another such blow. Besides, she *wanted* to be Mrs.

Frederick Wentworth. For the past eight years, she had wanted little else.

For a moment, Frederick feared Anne might reject his offer because of the "other fellow" Charles Musgrove had mentioned and was relieved when she asked where they would live."

"Here at Kellynch. Apparently, Sophie finds you an excellent companion and is eager to have you stay. We certainly would not be squashed up in a house of that size."

"No," Anne said, laughing. "We would not."

"So, Anne Elliot, what is your answer to my proposal?"

"My answer is that I accept the offer of your hand in marriage, and I shall do everything within my power to make you a good wife."

"That is all I ask," Frederick responded, taking her hand and kissing it. "Shall we go to Bath so that I might ask your father's consent?"

"No," Anne answered with a ferocity that surprised her betrothed. *I made that mistake once; I shall not do it again.* "It is not necessary. I am twenty-seven years old and capable of making up my own mind."

"Then if you will choose the day, I shall ask my brother, Edward, to marry us. Is that agreeable?"

"Yes, Frederick, it is," Anne said, addressing him by his Christian name for the first time since they had parted in '06. "Would Christmas day be agreeable? That will give the vicar sufficient time to publish the banns."

"Christmas Day. New Year's Day. Twelfth Night. Whatever day you choose is acceptable to me," Frederick answered. "And may I suggest you wear your blue dress? You look lovely in it."

"I shall be happy to accommodate you," she answered, pleased that he had taken notice of her efforts.

"Shall we return to the house where we can share our good news with my sister and Admiral Croft?"

"Yes, but I do not think it will come as a surprise, at least not to Mrs. Croft. She is staring out the dining room window in our direction." Both laughed and made haste to Kellynch Hall.

Chapter 8

"Anne, I have heard the most alarming report," a breathless Lady Russell said as soon as she was seated in the drawing room at Kellynch.

"And what report would that be?" Although Anne asked the question, she already knew the answer. Mrs. Manning, the vicar's wife, had written to Lady Russell of the approaching nuptials, thus the reason why the lady was sitting in a drawing room at Kellynch and not in her rooms in Bath.

"That you are to marry Captain Wentworth."

"Why would that report cause alarm?"

"Anne, you know as well as I do that the captain and you have a past."

"And apparently a future," Anne answered firmly, refusing to give way to the older woman. She had done that once before, and she could hardly bear to think of what it had cost her. "Considering I am a spinster with little fortune and no prospects, I thought you would be pleased to learn I am to marry a respectable man of position and wealth."

"But that is why I have hurried here. You are not without prospects. Your cousin, William Elliot, heir to Kellynch, has reconciled with your father. He is now a widower and is determined to marry an Elliot."

"Then I am happy for Elizabeth. After all, it was she who was destined to marry the heir to Kellynch Hall and be addressed as Lady Elliot, not I."

Lady Russell made a sour face, something she did whenever Anne rejected her role as counselor. But Anne, at twenty-seven, thought very differently from what she had been made to think at nineteen, and she would not yield on this matter.

"Apparently, Mr. Elliot is not interested in Elizabeth. It seems he finds her sharp tongue to be off-putting and disapproves of her association with Mr. Shepherd's daughter, Mrs. Clay."

Disapproves of Mrs. Clay? Of course, William Elliot would disapprove of Mrs. Clay, a lady who was working hard to secure the affections of the baronet. After all, if Papa were to take a wife and father a son, Mr. Elliot would no longer be the heir to Kellynch. But in this, Mr. Elliot was mistaken. Her father had no interest in marrying anyone. Why should he? Elizabeth and dear Papa were cut from the same cloth. In fact, her father had much more in common with his eldest daughter than he had ever had with his wife. As for Mrs. Clay, the only reason Sir Walter tolerated the company of a woman who should have been beneath his notice was that her excessive praise and fawning attention pumped him up. There was nothing the Master of Kellynch admired more than an acquaintance acknowledging the sun rose and set upon his shoulders.

"Although Elizabeth has made a poor impression," Lady Russell continued, "Mr. Elliot has memories of your kindness and has mentioned you frequently in conversation."

Anne assured Lady Russel that she was pleased to hear that Mr. Elliot had good memories of their brief time together, but it would not change her mind regarding her marriage to Captain Wentworth.

"If you marry Mr. Elliot, you will be Lady Elliot, and you will be able to stay at your beloved Kellynch for the rest of your life."

Anne already knew of Mr. Elliot's attempt to mend fences as Elizabeth had written to her in detail about the handsome William Elliot who was in regular attendance at Camden Place. After reading her sister's letters, Anne had tried to recall the man. But all that came to mind were faded memories of a shameless flatterer who peppered his speech with superlatives, especially when addressing her father. Furthermore, titles carried little weight with her, and although she loved Kellynch, at some point in the future, she hoped to be settled away from Somerset, preferably occupying a house near the sea.

Hoping that this discussion would come to a conclusion, Anne did not respond to Lady Russell's comments because the outcome was not in doubt. She would *never* marry Mr. Elliot.

"I believe the reason for your refusal to consider Mr. Elliot is because you have been taken in by Mrs. Croft's stories. She has romanticized her voyages with Admiral Croft and lured you in. The admiral's wife makes the crossing of the Atlantic sound like a picnic in the park when you and I have friends who have written of the horrific trans-Atlantic voyages they endured, and ships *do* go to the bottom of the sea."

"At this point, all discussion about the navy is irrelevant. As you know, the captain is retired."

"Quite right. As you say, the captain is retired, and there will be no more prize ships. The fortune he has now is all the money he will ever have."

"Lady Russell, you know me to be a person who requires little in the way of material goods. But to satisfy your concerns, I know how shares in prize ships are divided. From newspaper accounts, I also know what ships Frederick brought into port. I can assure you he is a man of considerable wealth. Can you say the same for Mr. Elliot? We know little of the man. For example, how much of his wife's fortune is left to him?"

But Anne's arguments would not deter the lady. Despite Frederick having made his mark and his fortune, Lady Russell had no intention of admitting she had erred when she had advised Anne to break the engagement with Captain Wentworth.

"Anne, you are of a sentimental nature. I think you have idealized the war hero to the point where he is larger than life."

"I can assure you I am *not* an adolescent worshiping at the altar of a naval hero," an annoyed Anne responded. "If I was taken in by anything, it was his character, not his heroics."

"Then what of Captain Wentworth's memory loss? There is the possibility he will never be fully whole again."

"It is true that, at present, some of the names and faces of people Frederick has known elude him, but please do not speak of him as not being *whole*. He has the full use of his reason and is a good and kind man. Do I not deserve such a person?"

"Of course, you do, and that is my purpose in coming here—to tell you of Mr. Elliot's interest. He is handsome, well-mannered, intelligent—"

"Forgive me for interrupting, Lady Russell, but as you continue to press, I must be blunt. Mr. Elliot's marriage to a lady of 'undue distinction,' to use my father's words, resulted in a schism between the two Elliot branches. Until recently, Mr. Elliot was content to have it so and made no attempt at reconciliation. And yet he goes to Bath determined to marry an Elliot. Why the sudden change of heart? Furthermore, I am curious as to the reasons for Mr. Elliot's interest in *me*. Our acquaintance is so limited. I wonder how he speaks of me at all. To be perfectly honest with you, I am suspicious of his motives. The question I must ask is: did Mr. Elliot spend all of his wife's fortune and looks for another, thus accounting for his renewed interest in our family?

"The only other thing I have to add to this discussion is a request that you counsel Papa to question in detail Mr. Elliot so that he might learn more about his heir. However, he should not do so on my behalf as *I* have no interest in the gentleman. We shall say no more on the subject as Captain Wentworth has returned from his morning ride."

Frederick came into the drawing room and greeted Lady Russell. For some reason, he did not like the woman, and he wondered why. Yes, she looked down her long nose at him, but others had done the same. Attempts by people of rank to diminish him because he was a self-made man never hit their mark. No, it was something else—something personal—but as he had no memory of her before his return to Somerset, it must remain a mystery.

"Captain Wentworth, please come in and join us. Lady Russell has heard our good news and has come to wish us joy."

"Yes, I have heard your news," Lady Russell said, rising, "and I am sure there is much to do in preparation for your wedding day, so I shall not detain you. I wish you joy and hope *this time* you and Anne will be happy."

"Thank you, Lady Russell," Frederick said, bowing.

After assisting Lady Russell to her carriage, Frederick turned to Anne and asked, "What did Lady Russell mean when she said she hoped I would be happy *this time?*"

Hearing Lady Russell's remark, Anne anticipated that Frederick would question her, and she had her answer at the ready. "Because you have no memory of your time at Kellynch, I did not wish to speak of it before. But because you have asked, I shall tell you. Eight years ago, before you took command of the *Asp*, you came here for a visit. At the time, my father was less than a gracious host. When you left, you were quite angry, and Lady Russell was a witness to the exchange."

Anne hoped Frederick would ask no additional questions. In answering, she had not lied. Her father *had been* rude in responding to the captain's request for his daughter's hand. Parroting Lady Russell's arguments, Sir Walter had stated that with Anne's claims of birth, beauty, and mind, she would be throwing herself away on a young man who had nothing but himself to recommend him and had little hope of attaining affluence in a most uncertain profession. Although she had not lied, she *had* skirted the truth. This was not a conversation Anne wished to repeat—ever.

"Of course, your father didn't want me here. I had not yet made my mark. I am sure he felt as if I were an intruder. Completely understandable."

"No, it is *not* understandable," Anne said, shaking her head vigorously. "You had already served your nation with courage and distinction. For that alone, you should have been welcomed with open arms. I am ashamed of how you were treated in our home and for my part in it as well. I should have been more firm in arguing on your behalf."

Frederick laughed. "But you were only nineteen at the time. I daresay if your father made the same complaint against me today that you would defend me with gusto. You certainly do not hesitate in arguing with *me*, and some of your arguments are compelling. In fact, you have actually convinced me to start reading novels and Shakespeare's plays. I have already begun a study of the Bard's *Julius Caesar*."

"You find only *some* of my arguments compelling? Obviously, you are in need of further instruction," Anne said, in a teasing voice, relieved that Frederick had not pressed her on the issue of his first visit to Kellynch. If he had asked, she would have been forced to tell the whole truth, and once he learned that she had broken his heart eight years earlier, what would he do? She really could not bear to think he might walk away from her again.

Chapter 9

Anne sat at her dressing table biting her thumb. It was a bad habit she had acquired after the death of her mother. Whenever she was nervous, she would nibble on the corner of her nail, and because she was so nervous about what was about to happen, her thumb was red and sore.

Earlier in the day, she had exchanged marriage vows with Captain Frederick Wentworth in the village church. Elegantly attired in a dark blue coat and tan breeches, he looked so handsome that he nearly took Anne's breath away, and he actually did when he told her that he had never seen a lovelier bride.

It had been such a beautiful day: cold, crisp, and nearly cloudless. Well wishers from the village stood at the church door and showered the couple with flower petals taken from Kellynch's conservatory. A lovely wedding breakfast with Mr. and Mrs. Croft, the

Reverend and Mrs. Wentworth, and the Musgroves followed. None of her relations had been invited as this was a day to rejoice and be glad. Anne had no wish to see the disappointed faces of her family.

Because everyone loved Anne, all her friends were happy that she had found someone to love, especially someone as highly regarded as Captain Frederick Wentworth. Included among the well wishers was Louisa Musgrove, who had secretly hoped the captain would make an offer to her, but who was pleased for her friend nonetheless.

During the wedding breakfast, Anne did not have a care in the world. Despite a rumor that she no longer danced, she stepped lively for a good part of the day while the Musgrove sisters took turns playing the piano-forte. But now the dancing would give way to something else entirely.

The marriage bed held no terror for Anne. After all, she would be with the man she had loved for nearly a decade. The problem was that Frederick did not love *her*. Instead of making love, they would come together for the purpose of procreation, reducing their union to its most basic elements.

Anne was trying to rid her mind of such thoughts when she heard Frederick's knock on the door connecting their two bedrooms, a signal he was ready to come to her. After taking one last look in the mirror, she went to the door and motioned for her husband, now in his dressing gown, to come in.

"You look lovely, Anne," Frederick said, admiring her green silk nightgown. He had no doubt Anne was nervous. To put her at ease, he took her by the hand and walked with her to the settee. "I have a wedding present for you." He handed Anne a receipt from a London auction house.

"You bought my mother's furniture," Anne said as she scanned the document. "Oh, Frederick, you could not have given me a better gift! I now own my mother's dressing table and wardrobe, and no one can ever take them away from me." She rewarded his kindness with a quick kiss on the lips, but it was enough to remind her of the many stolen kisses they had shared and the pleasure they had given her when they were experiencing the first bloom of love.

"Is there anything you want to talk about, Anne?"

"No, thank you. It is not necessary. I spoke to your sister. She was very helpful. I know what is expected."

"I am glad to hear it, but I was referring to our wedding breakfast," Frederick said, laughing.

"Oh!" Anne said in full blush. "The breakfast was wonderful. It has been so long since I feasted on such a banquet."

"You hardly ate a thing," Frederick said, and he took her hand in his. "You were too busy biting your thumbs."

"You do not miss a thing, do you?"

"It is part of my training as a naval officer. My memory in that regard is quite good. I only wish it was equally good in remembering the men I served with."

"I am convinced that in time your memory will be restored," Anne said, covering his hand with hers. "It was only a few days ago you mentioned a conversation you had with Sophia when you were children together at Monkton. It is possible these fragments may eventually come together to create a whole picture."

"Well, since the navy wants none of me, it really does not matter. What does matter is that today I begin a new life with you."

Frederick took Anne's hand and led his wife to the bed and gestured for her to get in. After removing his dressing gown, he joined her. Taking her in his arms, he kissed her forehead and whispered that he hoped he would never do anything that would hurt her. And then he kissed her mouth and found that she responded without hesitation as if she had been waiting for such a thing her whole life. As his hand traced the outline of her figure and reached under her nightgown, she was equally responsive to his touches.

Upon entering her, he waited for some indication that he was hurting her. Instead, he found her responding to his every movement. After making her his own, he realized this poor creature had been so starved for affection that even something so new, so intensely personal, was welcomed when compared to the coldness she had experienced while living amongst the Elliots of Kellynch Hall.

After seeing to her toilette, Anne returned to bed, hoping that Frederick would again take her in his arms, and when he did, she rested her head upon his chest. Although Anne quickly fell asleep, Frederick could not. Instead of being content with the first time Anne and he had come together as man and wife, he was highly agitated. He arose from the bed and went to the window and found, strangely enough, that he was flooded with restored memories of his childhood, most especially of his father, who had died when Frederick was eleven years old. Unlike his mother, who had passed away when he was only six, at least he remembered the man, especially when he patted the young Frederick on his head, the last tender gesture he would experience as a boy. A year after his father's passing, having failed in his efforts to secure an apprenticeship for Frederick on one of His Majesty's ships, his guardian had made arrangements for him to attend the naval academy in Portsmouth.

The goal of the academy was to turn boys into men—sailors into officers—and it had succeeded. Despite the harsh discipline and Spartan regimen, Frederick had excelled, and his leadership skills were clearly in view. After putting out to sea, he continued to distinguish himself. While serving as an ensign on the HMS *Donegal*, he had been promoted to the rank of lieutenant, but his opportunity to show what he was made of came at the Battle of Santo Domingo. His reward for his actions: command of the *Asp* at an age when most young men were still kissing the posteriors of their captains.

After chasing the French fleet across the Atlantic, Frederick returned to Somerset where he was hailed as a hero by his young brother and lauded by his neighbors for his derring-do on the high seas. His success opened doors for him with the gentry, and he soon found himself on the guest list of families who had not known of his existence when he had lived amongst them. And because of his local celebrity, he had received an invitation to visit Kellynch Hall.

Now I remember going to Kellynch. I was greeted by Elizabeth Elliot. No, that's not right. I was first introduced to an older woman—perhaps Lady Russell as Anne's mother would have already been dead. She was very gracious and walked with me into the gardens where I was introduced...

He had been so lost in thought that he did not hear his wife get out of bed. "Frederick, is something wrong?" Anne asked, placing her hand gently on his arm.

"No, not at all. I was restless. Please go back to bed. You will catch your death."

"It is not *that* cold in here. I am more concerned about you. You seem so...so unsettled."

"Oh, I see how it will be. *You* are so observant that I shant be able to get anything past *you*," he said, trying to avoid her probing look.

"Then something *is* wrong."

"No. Yes. I don't know," Frederick stuttered in frustration at the loss of his memory. Clearly distressed, he ran his hand through his thick black hair. "I can't explain it, Anne. Everything is such a jumble. Sometimes I feel as if my memory is just out of reach. If I could take but one more step, I would emerge from this dense fog that enshrouds me. I am close..so close. I know I am."

"My darling, perhaps you are trying too hard. The things you have remembered have come to you without effort. It is when you *seek* them out that your memories remain out of reach."

"Of course, as usual, you are right. You are a wise women, Anne Elliot. I mean, Anne Wentworth," Frederick said, squeezing her hand. "I fear I will win few arguments with you."

"Then let us never argue," Anne said, tugging at his arm so he might return to bed.

"Yes, let us never argue. Furthermore, I shall take your advice. Rather than seek them, I shall let my memories come to me."

"Better than old memories are new ones, and we shall have our share," Anne said, and she stood on her toes and kissed her husband on his cheek. After returning to bed, they welcomed a new day by making love.

Chapter 10

When the newlyweds were together, the conversation sparkled and Anne's wit and girlish laugh brightened Frederick's day. But when she was not with him, his thoughts were dark, betraying a restlessness within him.

"Are you happy, Frederick?" Sophia asked as she watched her brother wear a path in the drawing room carpet.

"Yes, of course. Anne is all I could want in a wife. I would spend every moment of the day with her if I could, but her duties as temporary housekeeper keep her busy. At this point, I do think Mrs. Leatherberry is taking advantage of her mistress by staying away for so long."

"Anne told me the poor woman has not had a day off in twelve years. Surely, she is entitled to visit her relations. Considering the time between visits and the distance, there is much catching up to do."

"Catching up? Really? What can a housekeeper possibly have to discuss? There is little difference in the day-to-day management of an estate. Change the linen, dust the furniture, beat the carpets, etc."

"I am sure Mrs. Leatherberry would not speak of such mundane tasks," Sophia said. "Rather, the housekeeper would share the peculiarities of Kellynch's inhabitants. Just think about Sir Walter and the makeup he applies or Mary Musgrove's feigned illnesses. Would not a discussion of those two Elliots result in an evening's entertainment in themselves?"

"You and I may laugh about Sir Walter waxing eloquent about Gowland's lotion or Mary's hypochondria, but Mrs. Leatherberry has been here for twenty years. Surely by this time, her relations knows the traits of the master and his daughters."

"You speak as a man, Frederick. Family life is always of greater interest to a woman. Besides, if you were with Anne every minute of every day, you would complain she was as idle as you are."

"Of course, you are right."

"But you *are* unsettled. Is there a specific reason?"

"Other than that I hate sitting on my...rear end all day?"

"Yes, other than that."

Sophia knew of Frederick's recurring dream of the lady in the meadow, and he had confessed to his sister that he had dreamt of her even on his wedding night. Despite efforts to rid his mind of her image, she reappeared night after night, just out of reach, and always facing away from him.

"By dreaming of another woman, I feel as if I am being unfaithful to Anne, and she certainly does not deserve that."

"You are being too hard on yourself. I am convinced this woman represents all that you lost when you were injured. This figment of your imagination has taken the place of those memories that remain beyond your reach."

"You do not think this mystery woman is my chestnut-haired beauty?"

"I would prefer to think of her as the woman you were destined to marry. In that case, the lady is Anne."

Frederick remained silent. He had grown to love Anne as she was kind and decent and worthy of his affection, but his love was not the passionate kind that inspired the romantic poets or those recorded in the great love stories of history. It was an everyday, utilitarian sort of love—one that in the end would serve him better as most of the great love stories ended in tragedy. But because he wanted more for Anne, he felt unworthy of his wife's greater love for him.

"Frederick, you have been married little more than a fortnight. I am sure your love will grow, especially with the birth of your children. I would suggest a honeymoon journey as soon as Mrs. Leatherberry returns."

"To Bath, perhaps, to see her family?"

"No, I would advise against that."

Sophia understood from Anne that news of her marriage had created a storm at Camden Place. Her father had responded to the announcement with a letter filled with accusations and invective. Because Sir Walter believed a union between the two Elliot branches would have eased his financial burdens, it had been his wish for Anne to wed her cousin, William Elliot. But her marriage to Wentworth had crushed all his hopes in that regard, and by marrying "that sailor," Anne had done a disservice to her eldest sister. Without familial ties to bind William Elliot to the family, Elizabeth would find it necessary to rely on the kindness of her relations after her father's death.

Sophia had watched as Anne folded the letter in disgust, and she knew what Anne was thinking. If the economies put in place by Lady Elliot at Kellynch Hall had been followed in the years subsequent to her death, Elizabeth would not now be so vulnerable. However, it was her father's statement that Elizabeth would be poorly treated that had rankled the most. Surely, Sir William knew Anne would never leave her sister destitute no matter how much she deserved it.

"Frederick, you do know that it was because Sir Walter was not consulted about the marriage that his feelings were hurt, but they will heal of that I am sure." Knowing the baronet would always exceed his income, Sophia had no doubt Sir Walter would find it necessary to look to his son-in-law to rescue him from his debtors. "As to your honeymoon, I would suggest you consult the bride about your destination and not your sister."

"Perhaps something by the sea," Frederick said.

Sophia knew that Anne, who would deny her husband nothing, would agree.

* * *

"Anne, where is my brush."

"On your dressing table," Anne called to her husband from her bedchamber.

93

"Not my hairbrush. The brush for my coat."

Anne opened a drawer on her dressing table and removed the clothes brush. "Since I have been serving in the capacity of valet, the brush was in my room where it has been since we were married. And this may be the perfect time for us to discuss the employment of a manservant."

"Do you have someone in mind?" Frederick asked, handing the brush back to Anne so she might remove the lint from his jacket.

"I do. One of our grooms, Jack Nettles."

"The groom with the light brown hair and pug nose? The one who serves us our supper every night?"

Anne nodded.

"But with such a name, he may turn out to be prickly by nature."

"How funny you are, Frederick. I am sure Nettles has never heard that comment before."

"But why Nettles?"

"When one of our household servants emigrated to North America, Mr. Allgood suggested that Jack, then a stable hand, be made a groom. Prior to our butler being whisked away to Bath, Jack was coming along nicely under Mr. Allgood's direction."

"Then why not train him for the position of butler? There is the possibility Mr. Allgood may never return from Bath."

"I already thought about that," Anne responded. "Although Jack is a fine lad, unfortunately, he is not very good with numbers and that is an absolute necessity for the position of butler. If it were not for Mr. Allgood's talents as a manager of the household accounts, the Elliots of Kellynch Hall would be in even worse shape than we are at present. Because the Crofts do so little entertaining, we can manage without a butler for the present. However, there is much for a manservant to do. If the same person saw to your bath and clothes, you would know where everything is."

"I do not think a valet is necessary. I can button my own buttons, Anne."

"And you can comb your own hair, that is, if only you would stop losing the comb and brush." Anne straightened the collar on Frederick's jacket. "I do not understand why you are arguing with me on this. When you were aboard ship, I am sure you had a man to attend to your personal needs."

"Yes, an ensign named Skyler."

Frederick uttered the ensign's name as if it was as familiar to him as his own. Although her husband missed the significance of his statement, Anne did not.

"Frederick, you remembered Skyler's name—and with no forced effort on your part."

"By Jove, I did," Frederick said, smiling. "It just came to me. Well, what do you know!"

This was not the first time such a thing had happened, but most resurrected memories were in some way connected to the navy. Because of this, when Frederick had suggested a honeymoon journey, she had taken the liberty of writing to an old friend of his who had leased a house in Lyme.

"Visit James Harville?" Frederick said. "Yes, I like that idea. He is a fine fellow and was an able captain before a leg injury from exploding ordnance forced him on shore. I have never been to Lyme, and I should like to go. The sea air will do me good. Will you make the necessary arrangements? Reserve a room at a nearby inn, etc. You know what to do."

"Yes, I shall see to the arrangements for a visit to Lyme in the same way that I see to everything else."

Frederick acknowledged her statement with a nod. "I shall strike a bargain with you. If you will write to Mrs. Leatherberry asking for her to return from her extended holiday, I shall employ Nettles as a valet. Are we agreed?"

"Yes. It is the perfect solution for both of us. I will admit I was growing tired of playing the role of housekeeper. As for you, just think how much time will be saved if only one person is made the guardian of the master's combs and brushes," she said, tapping his chest with her finger.

"You are a saucy girl."

Anne laughed. She thought of the many descriptives that applied to her, but saucy was not one of them. But then Frederick slipped his arms around her waist and kissed her neck.

"May I sleep with you tonight?"

"You need not ask, Frederick. You may come to me whenever you want. I *am* your wife."

"Yes, you are my wife," and he kissed her gently, "and an excellent one. I thank you for that, Anne."

"I love you, Frederick," she said, placing her hand on his cheek.

"Yes, I know."

Chapter 11

As promised, Anne saw to all the accommodations for their honeymoon journey. As so few visitors came to Lyme in the winter, they were able to reserve a suite of rooms at The Three Cups, one that provided an excellent view of the Cobb and Channel.

Because Frederick was so eager to visit with the Harvilles, he would not let Anne unpack their clothes or to have a rest before venturing out, reminding her that she had slept in the carriage. Although Anne had closed her eyes, due to the roughness of the road, she had not nodded off, but she knew she was at risk of being lectured about letting the day go to waste if she did not immediately set out for the home of the Harvilles, even though it was starting to rain.

After arming his wife with an umbrella, the pair set off in the direction of the Cobb. As soon as Frederick felt the salt spray on his face and listened to the seagulls squawking their complaints, Anne witnessed a transformation. Her husband was no longer a country gentleman, but a seafaring man with saltwater in his veins.

"Why now blow wind, swell billow, and swim bark! The storm is up and all is on the hazard," the former sailor said while addressing his oration to an offshore squall. Anne wondered, if in all Frederick's enthusiasm for the view, did he realize he was quoting Shakespeare and that a piece of his memory had fallen into place?

It was a harder rain that finally drove the couple from the Cobb. Seeking shelter, they set out to find shelter at the home of Captain Harville. When they did locate it at the foot of a pier, they found it to be a small house of uncertain date, and squashed up inside this humble abode was Captain and Mrs. Harville and their brood of four. Anne and Frederick soon discovered that what they lacked in square footage, the Harvilles made up for in domestic felicity.

As soon as Anne and Frederick were inside the house, Frederick let out a cry, "Benwick! What the devil are you doing here?" he asked as he shook the hand of his former first officer.

"I am visiting with Captain Harville," Benwick answered.

Word of Wentworth's injury had made the rounds of those establishments frequented by naval officers who had been put on shore when Napoleon had been exiled to Elba. After learning that Wentworth was coming to Lyme, he had warned Benwick that his friend had lost a good part of his memory in an accident aboard the *Laconia*.

"The reason I am here is because I was engaged to Harville's sister Fanny," Benwick gently reminded his friend. "We were to marry after my return from the Cape."

"Please allow me to offer my belated congratulations. But where is your intended? I would like to meet her."

After a prolonged silence, Benwick explained that Fanny had died the previous year.

Frederick immediately apologized for his gaffe. "I am sorry, Benwick. If I knew of Fanny's passing, I have forgotten it." After explaining his injury, he added, "My loss of memory is the only excuse I have."

"Do not worry about it, Captain," Benwick said, slapping Wentworth on the back. "It is now more than a year since Fanny's passing, and although the wound heals slowly, I am doing better since coming to Lyme. But speaking of wounds, Harville was telling me that because of your injury you were unable to remember the names of those with whom you had served. I think he must have got it wrong because you knew me right away."

"Well, there are many faces whom I have forgotten, but I could never forget one as ugly as yours," Wentworth said, laughing. "Anne, Anne, come here. Allow me to introduce you to Captain James Benwick who served as my first lieutenant on the *Laconia* before being awarded his own command."

"You are a married man, Wentworth?" Benwick asked genuinely surprised. "Harville did not say."

"That is because Harville wanted to surprise you," Stephen Harville said as he stepped from behind Benwick and shook the hand of his comrade in arms. "Wentworth, do you remember my wife, Mrs. Harville?"

Without hesitation, Frederick answered, "I do, indeed. Mrs. Harville, please allow me to introduce you to my bride." The two ladies exchanged bows. "Anne, these are my former partners in crime: Captain Benwick and Captain Harville. Although Harville stole many a ship away from the French, Jane is Harville's greatest prize."

Anne was warmly greeted by Frederick's navy brethren and was made to feel as welcome as any actual member of their clan would have been. After agreeing to dine with the Harvilles, Benwick suggested the party walk on the Cobb while supper was being prepared. When Frederick learned the topic to be discussed was the romantic poets, he touched the scar on his head indicating his injury prevented him from engaging in such a heady discussion.

Anne wagged her finger at her husband. "You are excused—this time—and it is only because I know that you and Captain Harville will speak of tacking sail and maneuvering ships that I agree, but I do not want you to think I am unaware that this is an attempt on your part to evade a discussion of Byron and Cowper."

As they walked the promenade, Anne savored her literary discussion with Captain Benwick, but quickly realized that all the verses he quoted were tender songs of hopeless agony brought on by a broken heart, clearly a response to the death of his beloved Fanny Harville. To counterbalance the maudlin, she recommended a larger allowance of prose in his daily study and suggested Fielding's novels and Shakespeare's comedies. She was also so bold as to suggest that Benwick leave the Harvilles' home so he might seek the fellowship of the gentler sex. Knowing the Musgroves were now in Bath, and thinking of Louisa in particular, Anne promised to write a letter of introduction if Captain Benwick should decide to decamp for a visit to that town. The bachelor immediately agreed to the scheme.

Supper was such a success that the parties made plans to meet again the following day, but this time, Anne insisted on spending more of the day with Mrs. Harville. As the wife of a navy captain, Anne believed Jane Harville was in a position to share with her the role a wife played while on board a frigate. Unfortunately, she was soon to learn her time aboard ship had been of short duration. Before they could get underway, Jane discovered she was with child.

"Knowing that some of the voyages lasted for longer than a year, it grieved me to watch the *Chatham* sail out of Plymouth," Jane confessed. "In fact, Admiral Nelson once boasted he had sailed the *Victory* from Spithead in May 1803 and returned in August 1805 without entering port, a period of two years and three months." The mere utterance of the name of Britain's greatest naval hero caused Jane to pause as a sign of respect. "Poor man! Shortly thereafter, he sailed for Trafalgar and was killed by a marksman."

"But were you on board long enough to have a taste of seafaring life?" Anne asked, eager for information about a woman's life aboard one of His Majesty's frigates.

"No," Jane answered. "I am sorry to disappoint you, but I was not. The day after I boarded the *Chatham*, the fleet was hit with a strong gale, and we could not get out of the harbor. In all the time I was on board ship, I was terribly seasick and never left the cabin. For eight days, the wind was against us. By the time they turned in our favor, I suspected it was more than a case of *mal de mer* I was experiencing. I was right; our son had snuck on board inside me." Jane Harville burst out laughing at the memory. "When I told Mr. Harville, he insisted I return to my family and rightly so. The next day, I was put in a boat and rowed to shore. We had only been married four months. But such is the life of a wife of a naval officer. You are fortunate in that Captain Wentworth has retired. You will not have to endure these tearful partings."

During the course of the day and over numerous cups of tea, Anne and Jane Harville formed a bond of friendship. Frederick watched in amusement as his wife listened to stories concerning the antics of the four Harville children. When seven-year-old Stephen shared his aspirations to become a captain in the navy just like his father, Anne stood up and saluted him, which delighted the youngster.

Upon their return to The Three Cups, Frederick remarked on the length of Anne's discussion with Mrs. Harville and asked what news they had shared.

"You would have no interest in our conversation. It was the equivalent of drawing room babble," Anne said, referencing his earlier remark. "Nonetheless, I thoroughly enjoyed it. I only wish I had had such ease of conversation with my own sisters. How differently things might have turned out."

"In order for you to have had a different outcome with your sisters, one of them would have had to stop talking long enough for you to make comment."

Despite Frederick having been in Elizabeth's company for only as long as it took the Crofts to sign the lease on Kellynch, he found her conversation to be filled with cutting remarks about those whom she considered beneath her, which included just about everyone in Somerset. And while the eldest Elliot daughter spewed venom, Mary droned on about perceived slights or her health or her in-laws. Sandwiched between two such unappealing characters, Frederick was amazed that Anne was as good a person as she was.

"Are we out of sorts this evening?" Anne asked after hearing Frederick's remark about her sisters.

"To the contrary. I am in excellent spirits as I have had good news." Frederick did not wait for Anne to ask him what his news was. "You know Napoleon escaped from his exile on Elba in February, and he has been marching north ever since."

Anne was aware of the former French emperor's activities because the newspapers were filled with stories of thousands of followers filling the ranks of a makeshift army marching toward Paris. Speculation had it that Napoleon would reach the French capital by late March.

"Well, it appears the Admiralty is recalling some of its officers. I am thinking about writing to Sir Joseph Yorke, Naval Lord, about being re-commissioned and given the command of the *Laconia*. What do you think, Anne?"

Frederick waited apprehensively for Anne's answer. When they had married, there had been no talk about the navy because his impaired memory prevented him from resuming his command, but now that his memory, at least as far as the navy was concerned, had been restored, there was no reason why he should not apply for a command position.

"I think you should do it," Anne said without hesitation.

"You understand it may mean lengthy separations as there will be times when it would be too dangerous for you to be on board."

"Yes, I know," Anne said, pleased by Frederick inferring that at some point she would join him aboard ship. "But you are a sailor, and being confined to the country has done nothing for you or your disposition," she teased. "Your request was not unexpected. I confess to eavesdropping on your conversations with Captain Benwick and Captain Harville about this very topic."

"Anne, you are the absolute best wife a man could ever want," he said, and he picked her up and swung her about. "If I am commissioned and acquit myself well, after the war, I might still have a career in the navy. Things are changing quickly, and it will take men who are open to new ideas to pilot these ships. And I am a new man. Since our marriage, I have been reborn."

Anne went to her portable writing desk. After placing a blank sheet of paper on the top of it, she offered Frederick a pen. "I believe you have a letter to write to Sir Joseph Yorke."

Chapter 12

After three days of rain, the sun once again put in an appearance, and a walk along the promenade was suggested. While Frederick offered Mrs. Harville his arm, her husband did the same for Anne. Despite cautions from her escort that he would bore her with stories of his journeys around the Cape or fighting near Toulon and Cadiz, Anne assured Captain Harville that she could not get enough of these tales and confessed to reading lengthy reports of naval engagements in the newspapers.

"If it is length you crave, then I am your man," Harville said with a laugh.

While Anne was being entertained with stories of heroic deeds executed on the high seas, Mrs. Harville was congratulating her companion on his choice of wife. "I don't think I have ever met anyone more agreeable than Mrs. Wentworth."

"I am very fortunate. Anne is everything a man could want in a wife."

"And where did you meet her?"

"At Kellynch Hall in Somerset. My sister Sophia is married to Admiral Croft. Once he was paid off by the navy, he thought he should become a country gentleman, and he has taken a year's lease on the manor house. Being cast ashore suits him as well as it suits me."

"How funny. Having sailed around the world, you needed to come back to your home county to find a wife."

"I hadn't thought of it in that way, but, yes, I did have to come home to find a bride. Quite a coincidence that we both hail from Somerset."

"Is it? Since Anne has been following your career from the time you took command of the *Laconia*, I assumed you were already acquainted."

"What do you mean 'following my career?'"

"Anne knows your entire history: every voyage, every engagement, every prize ship taken. If there are things you have forgotten about your career, Captain, all you need do is ask your wife."

This exchange puzzled Frederick. He couldn't imagine why Anne would follow his career. Except for their brief acquaintance in '06, of which he had no recollection, he had not been in her company in eight years. Perhaps his being a local man had piqued her interest about his exploits. But in their many discussions about the navy, why had she given no hint that this was information she already knew?

"I suspect any article about my capturing a prize ship was accompanied by a sketch. Who could resist such a handsome face?" the captain said in a mocking tone. "However, I am a little surprised to hear of Anne's interest in the navy. It is certainly unique in her family. In fact, her father, Sir Walter Elliot, can barely tolerate being in the company of naval officers: 'coarse, brown men—the color of his livery,' he called us."

Without warning, Mrs. Harville stopped. "Your wife's maiden name is Elliot? Mrs. Wentworth is Anne Elliot of Kellynch Hall?"

Frederick nodded. "Do you know the family?"

"I don't. The Harvilles do not travel in the same circles as the Elliots, but then the family lives less than twenty miles away, so I would expect to hear news of them every now and then."

"Perhaps you read in the newspaper that Sir Walter and his daughter Elizabeth have recently taken rooms in Camden Place in Bath."

"Yes, of course, that is it exactly. If you don't mind, I think I'll catch up to Mrs. Wentworth." After doing so, Jane suggested to Anne that they walk back to the house together. Once in the house, Jane informed Anne that she had been ignorant of the fact that she was Anne Elliot of Kellynch Hall.

"Have we met before, Jane? Because if we have, I apologize for not remembering the acquaintance."

"No, I have never *met* you. But for the past eight years, I have known *of* you."

Anne shook her head in confusion.

"What I know of you came from Captain Wentworth."

"Frederick? I do not understand."

"Nine years ago, when Stephen and I were courting, Frederick teased him unmercifully about how Harville was acting because he was so in love with me. Frederick swore there was no woman on earth who could elicit such a response from him. But he was soon eating humble pie. A few months later, in a letter sent to us shortly after we had married, Frederick confessed it was his time to be teased as he had found an angel from heaven in Somerset. Although he wrote extensively of her character, beauty, and wit, he did not mention her name until he was next in our company. But by that time..."

"...it was all over," Anne said, finishing Jane's sentence.

"Yes," Jane answered in a sad voice. "When I questioned him, he told me the reason you had broken the engagement was your family's objections to the marriage. I tried to help, telling him that because you were of such a young age, you would naturally look to your family for guidance. I suggested that once he had proved himself he should try again. But he was angry and deeply wounded and heard little of what I had to say."

"Thank you for that, Jane. But nothing you could have said would have changed his mind. He was quite disgusted with my behavior. He had expected to marry a woman with a strong mind—not someone who was weak and timid and subservient to her family," Anne said, staring off into the distance.

"And he knows nothing of your prior engagement?"

"No, I did not tell him, and if you want to know why, it is because I am selfish. I have lived the past eight years in a lonely corner of Kellynch Hall without love or affection from my family of any kind. Having rejected a proposal from the only other man in the county who was in a position to make me an offer, I resigned myself to spinsterhood. But then the Crofts and Frederick came to Kellynch, and we were thrown into each other's company on a daily basis. We fell so easily into conversation. It was an absolute delight to be with him once again.

"Even so, when Frederick asked me to marry him, I was stunned. Anne Elliot, twenty-seven years old, past her bloom, noticed by no one, to be the wife of Captain Frederick Wentworth? Impossible! But then he gave me his reasons. He said he wanted a family, and since he found me to be a woman of steady character and sweetness of temper, he proposed. And I thought, why should I not accept him? Why should I not have some happiness in my life?"

Seeing the tears in Anne's eyes, Jane quickly responded. "Of course, you have the right to be happy. But what if Frederick remembers that you once broke his heart?"

"Since he proposed, that possibility has been constantly on my mind. From the time of our arrival in Lyme, inspired by the company of his naval comrades, many of Frederick's memories *have* returned. But other than some reminiscences from his earliest childhood, few of the memories are of a personal nature. At some future time, they may come back to him, but for the time being, all is well. And if he were to find out, I have reason to believe he will forgive me. You see, Jane, I am to have his child."

Jane had no time to respond as the men were approaching.

"Two women speaking in hushed tones," Frederick said as he came into the front room, "that always makes me nervous."

"Then you must have a guilty conscience, Captain Wentworth," Jane said, "as women are frequently given to whispering because men have decided that ladies must speak softly or risk having unflattering things said about them."

"Jane has you there, Wentworth," Captain Harville said. "You cannot complain unless you want a loud, brash woman welcoming you home."

"Then you will hear no complaint from me," Frederick answered, holding up his hands. "Mrs. Harville, it is unfortunate we are returning to Kellynch in the morning as Anne will surely miss your company, especially since my sister has written to me to say the admiral and she have gone to Bath. Apparently, Admiral Croft was so bored in the country he agreed to accompany his wife to Bath so that she might visit the shops. A desperate man indeed."

"Will you join them in Bath?" Mrs. Harville asked.

"No, Anne will not allow me anywhere near her relations for fear I will embarrass myself and her with my outspoken opinions."

"Nonsense, Frederick," Anne said emphatically. "You know it is the opposite I fear: that my family will say something that will embarrass *them*. However, your wish to be welcomed into the bosom of my family may be granted soon enough. It seems I am in my father's good graces once again."

Frederick looked at her with a quizzical brow.

"When I returned to The Three Cups yesterday, a letter from Mr. Allgood awaited me. Apparently, my concerns that my cousin, William Elliot, might be up to a bit of no good proved prescient. After some inquiries were made, it was learned that the future heir to Kellynch is totally bankrupt. It seems there is nothing left of his wife's fortune as he gambled it all away, and debt collectors have followed him to Bath, thus exposing him as a scoundrel."

"And by marrying you, he thought he would be able to tap into your father's reserves," Frederick said. "Little did he know he would have found a dry keg."

"I would ask that you not repeat what has just been said," Anne said to the Harvilles, "as it would be great embarrassment to my family to have such a revelation become public knowledge."

"You can count on us. Besides, there are few families who do not have secrets," Jane answered. "I hope you will always regard me as your confidante."

"Are you implying, Mrs. Harville, there are other secrets to be learned about Anne?" Frederick asked, looking askance at his wife. "If so, I am curious to know what they are."

"Well, they wouldn't be secrets if we told you," Anne answered and went into the kitchen, leaving her husband behind with a puzzled look on his face.

While Anne was in the next room, Jane begged a word with the captain, and they walked out onto a porch so their conversation could not be overheard.

"I can see you are very happy with your choice of bride, so what I am about to say is rather difficult."

"Speak freely, ma'am. There is no need to pick and choose your words with me. I know your motives are good."

"Very well. Many years ago, you loved another, and you shared with me the profound hurt you felt when the lady rejected you at the behest of her family."

"My sister has mentioned this grand passion I had for a lady with chestnut hair and blue eyes," Frederick said, turning his gaze on the waves crashing against the shore. "Although my visit to Lyme has worked upon my memory and some fragments of my past personal life have been jarred loose, the picture remains incomplete. It seems the wound inflicted by this young woman was so profound, my mind continues to hide the details of our affair. But it no longer matters as I now have Anne."

"Is it possible you and Anne were destined for each other—that through some higher plan you were meant to marry Anne Elliot?"

"I do not know if I can agree that a higher power has taken an interest in the romantic inclinations of two ordinary people." Seeing the look of concern on Jane's face, Frederick added, "I know in these past two weeks you and Anne have become friends, and I am pleased to have it so. I do not want you to worry about my wife as I appreciate her more than you could ever know."

"Yes, do appreciate her, Frederick" Jane said, taking his hand. "But you must also love and cherish her."

"I do, Jane. I do. It was not always the case, but when I came here and saw how happy you and Stephen are, I realized that this is something I have as well. I have come to believe that it has been there from the beginning."

"But, Frederick, there are different kinds of love. The love of which I speak is the kind that binds a couple together so they might weather any storm."

"You have no worries on that account. I do love Anne. I love her so very dearly."

"Then tell her every day of her life. Those words cannot be spoken enough," Jane said. "Well, I have said my piece, so let us go in. There's a stew on the fire."

Frederick gestured for the lady to go ahead of him. Before joining the others, he needed to collect his thoughts. He was convinced Jane Harville had been trying to tell him something about his past—something about the girl he had once loved—and somehow all these things were tied to Anne.

Chapter 13

On the journey to Kellynch, Anne felt the weight of the secret she had carried since Frederick proposed. After speaking with Jane Harville, she knew she should have told Frederick the truth. By not doing so, she had committed the sin of omission. But the reason for her silence was her hope that over time Frederick would come to love her in her new incarnation, but that had not happened—certainly not in the way of lovers. Although he spoke of affection, respect, and admiration, he had never said, "I love you." Despite his failure to utter those words, she had freely declared her love for him. In doing so, she hoped to overwhelm him by the depth of her love and that he would love her in return.

But in order for Anne and Frederick to go forward, it required a visit to the past. To continue on as they were was to live a lie, and Anne could no longer do that, especially now that she was expecting his child.

Anne waited in her bed for Frederick to come to her. Even when they did not make love, he preferred to sleep with her, and she often found him curling up against her during the night to the point where his body took her shape. Even though she often found it difficult to sleep with him breathing in her ear, she made no complaint. They had eight years of separation to make up for.

After slipping beneath the bed covers, Frederick ran his hand across her belly. For a moment, Anne wondered if he knew about the baby, but no, it was a prelude to other things. His hand was soon under her nightgown, and as her passion rose, she pulled him on top of her and moved his manhood against her. When she was ready, she placed him inside her and felt his thrust as he sought her depths. After placing her hands on his buttocks, she pulled him deeper still. And then she heard his soft moan signaling his release and felt his body collapsing upon hers.

As she did every time after they had made love, Anne ran her hands up and down his back. On a few occasions, the gentle touches had lulled him to sleep, and she would feel his full weight upon her. But not tonight. While she traced the outline of the curvature of his spine with her fingers, he whispered, "I love you, Anne."

Upon hearing those words, Anne flinched, and Frederick could feel her tighten around his manhood, and he rolled off of her and pulled her onto his chest.

"I know you are surprised to hear those words, but I assure you I *do* mean them. I should have told you sooner, but these feelings have been coming on so gradually. And now I feel as if a dam has been breached, and the waters flow freely. And I shall make you a promise: You will hear those three words every day of your life, and if we are parted, I shall write the words and send them to you by post."

In her imagination, Anne had enacted many a scene where Frederick had professed his love for her, but none was as wonderful as this gentle scene.

"Oh, Frederick, thank you for loving me," she said, sitting up, "but there is something I must tell you."

Anne fumbled for the right words. She started and stopped and started again, but the words she needed to explain what she had done would not come. Finally, her courage deserted her. *No, I cannot do it. Not tonight. Not after he told me how much he loves me.*

"Is something wrong?" Frederick asked. "You are not ill, are you?"

"No, Frederick. I am quite well. Better than I had expected considering…"

"Considering what?" Frederick asked with alarm.

"…considering that I am to have a baby."

"A baby?" Frederick was stunned. "I am to be a father?"

"Yes. If I am to be a mother, then you must be a father."

Frederick sat up and pulled Anne to him. "When?"

"I imagine in about seven months."

"Will it be a boy or a girl?"

"Frederick, I am an expectant mother not a seer."

"Of course you aren't," he said, laughing at his ridiculous question. "Oh, I knew when I asked you to marry me that all would be well. It could not have been any other way as you are such a kind person, and because of your caring nature, I was determined to make you a good husband."

"And you have. All I ask is that you love me and forgive me for any transgressions or shortcomings."

"Transgressions? I know of none. Shortcomings? You do not have any. You are so perfect that I pale in comparison."

"Then may I ask your indulgence for any transgressions that may come to your attention in the future."

"Anne, I believe you are incapable of doing wrong. If you have done something I would disagree with, I may question what you did, but never your motives. Does that satisfy?"

Anne nodded. She only hoped he would feel the same way in the morning.

Chapter 14

When Frederick came down to breakfast, he was in his riding clothes, and he asked his wife if she would join him.

"You can still ride, can't you, Anne? I mean, with the baby and all," Frederick asked while squeezing her hand. After again making love, Frederick had kept his wife up half the night so that they might talk about this miracle growing inside her. He was so excited by her news that he confessed it was his intention to embarrass himself by telling everyone he knew and every passerby he encountered that he was to be a father.

Anne laughed at his exaggerated statements and wondered if all men reacted in such a way to the news of the impending arrival of their first child.

"I am sure I can still ride," Anne reassured him, "but not this morning. Before going to Lyme, I checked the medicine cupboard and found we are lacking in just about everything. It is my intention to walk into the village and visit the apothecary for the purpose of replenishing our supplies."

"Walk? Why will you not take the carriage? Ferris can take you into the village."

"Yes, Ferris can take me, but I shall not ask him. As you well know, I *like* to walk. And since Mrs. Leatherberry is now at the helm once again, I shall be able to do more of it."

"And how will you go?"

"The same way I always go. I shall take the path through the meadows and enter the village near the church. On my way home, I shall stop and visit the vicar and his wife."

"Oh, if you are to visit the vicar, then I shall have a leisurely ride as you will not be home for hours."

"Frederick, do be kind," Anne said, gently chastising her husband. She knew he found the vicar's sermons dull and his wife's conversation on a par with her husband's homilies. Every Sunday, he fidgeted in church, much as a boy of ten would have, and there was nothing subtle about it.

"The man is older than Methuselah. He should retire."

"You would wish Mr. Manning to be put out to pasture? You did not like it when the navy did it to you."

"Put out to pasture? That is a terrible metaphor for a sailing man. And, yes, I *should* be kind, but I have no patience for sermons or dining on tea cakes while the Mannings speak of Mrs. Myrtle's gout or Mr. Grover's goiter."

"And that is why your brother chose to take orders while you preferred the sea."

Rising from her chair, she kissed her husband on the cheek, but before she could step away from him, he slipped his hands around her waist. "Today, I did not tell you I loved you, and last night, I promised a day would not go by without me saying those words. So, my dear, I love you."

"You told me you loved me when the sun was just coming up," she said, giving him a gentle punch on the shoulder. "You woke me up for that very purpose."

"Among other things," Frederick said, nuzzling her breasts.

"Frederick, the servants are about," she said, gently pushing him away. But he ignored her warning and pulled her onto his lap. As her husband was in an excellent frame of mind, she thought she might mention there was something she needed to tell him and requested an audience when she returned from the village.

"You sound so serious, Anne."

"It is just something I neglected to mention, and I want to get it out into the open."

"My goodness, Mrs. Wentworth! Are you confessing to a love affair?"

Anne blushed. "Goodness no! But even so, the answer will surprise you." After kissing him once again, she left him to his breakfast.

* * *

After mounting Galahad, Frederick took off at a brisk pace. There was nothing on land quite like putting a horse through its paces. Each morning, he would ride through Kellynch's meadows at a gallop, shouting a greeting to the laborers who were already preparing the fields for spring planting. When he needed to rest Galahad, he would trot through the village, waving to those he encountered as they prepared to open their shops for business.

Anne understood Frederick's need to move his body as he was not a man to sit idly about the house reading novels, and since their visit to Lyme, he realized that the life of a country squire was not for him. At the very least, Anne and he must take a lease on a house near the sea. He needed to see ships at anchor, smell the salt in the air, feel the sand in the wind, and hear the crashing of the waves upon a rocky shore.

Even better than living near the sea would be to sail upon it. He longed for a command, but all his hopes in that area depended upon the Admiralty. But why should he not have a favorable response from them? He was a damned fine captain, and knowing that most of the frigates were being refitted with armor plates, during his months on shore, he had made it a point to educate himself on the technological advances being made in shipbuilding. With much of his memory restored, he thought he might actually be given a command. In the meantime, the days loomed long before him, that is, when he wasn't with Anne.

As he slowed to a trot, Frederick thought about his bride. Since discovering he was actually in love with his wife, a sense of wellbeing had filled him to the point where he was walking about the house like a boy with his first crush. And because he was so deeply in love, their lovemaking had taken on a new depth. The previous night, despite her news, he found he could not leave her alone. *Not that she seemed to mind,* Frederick thought, and he was pleased Anne enjoyed such intimacies.

After returning from his ride and stabling Galahad, he was met at the door of the manor by his newly appointed manservant.

"Nettles, I worked up a real sweat today. I shall need a bath"

Nettles answered that he would see to it immediately, but before leaving him to his work, Frederick thought he should talk to the young man about what was required of a valet in his service and gestured to Nettles that he should follow him into the study.

"Mrs. Wentworth tells me you started out here at Kellynch in the stables." As soon as he uttered the statement, Frederick realized he already knew the lad. "Blast! I remember you. Whenever I visited Kellynch, you always saddled that splendid stallion for me. What was his name?"

"Mars was his name, sir. You told me he was the Roman God of War and the perfect horse for an officer going off to fight the French."

"Yes, Mars. An excellent mount. He had that beautiful chestnut coat."

"Yes, sir," Nettles said, smiling. He knew of the captain's loss of memory and was pleased to find it was returning. "When you went out riding with Miss Anne, as she was then called, you used to tease her that she and Mars had the same color mane, a beautiful chestnut. Mrs. Wentworth had a lot more red in her hair when she were younger."

"Miss Anne had chestnut hair. Is that what you just said?" Frederick asked.

Nettles nodded.

Frederick rose and went to the window. After looking in the direction of the meadows, everything came into focus. It was as if a windy day had cleared every cloud from the sky, and there was nothing to block his view. Standing in the vista before him was a beautiful young girl with chestnut-colored hair, blue eyes, and a gentleness about her that had touched his heart. He could see the two of them walking hand in hand through the meadows, occasionally stopping for a quick kiss, followed by Anne laughing at their brashness and wondering what people would say if they saw the two of them kissing. He had replied that every man in the shire would be jealous.

But then he remembered another walk—to the gazebo—where his lady love had told him she should not have accepted his offer of marriage before speaking to her father and she must break the engagement. But he had stubbornly refused to let her go. Knowing of her ill treatment at the hands of her family, Frederick understood her family's objections had more to do with keeping Anne at Kellynch than his inferior position in society or his naval career. He promised to take her away from the daily strife of living with a selfish father and two equally inconsiderate sisters. If she consented to the marriage, he would place her on a pedestal. But his efforts were too little and too late. When he finally realized she would bow to her family's demands, his shock had turned to anger, and he had spoken words so unkind that they had reduced her to tears and that was how he had left her.

Cast adrift by Anne's rejection, Wentworth had turned his full attention to making a success of his career. His single-mindedness in pursuing prize ships had made him a wealthy man, and his riches and fame attracted the attention of the well-heeled. As a result, his name appeared on the guest lists of the elite of society. Instead of being the son of a minister, he was the dashing, handsome, and very rich Captain Wentworth who could tell a ripping good tale of engagements fought and sea battles won. Between his newly made riches and his reputation for adventure on the high seas, his company was sought out by the daughters of aristocrats as well as families who had made their fortunes in trade. But the parade of beauties did nothing for him because he no longer had a heart. It had been ripped out of his chest when the only woman he could ever love had turned away from him.

"Sir, have I said something wrong?" a worried Nettles asked.

"No, you have not. But many years ago, *I* said something wrong, and I have been paying for it ever since."

Chapter 15

Frederick immediately left the house and went in search of Anne. He had walked half the distance to the village when he saw his wife coming down the path that cut through the meadows. The scene before him was as familiar to him as the inside of his cabin on the *Laconia*. For the past six months, he had seen a young lady standing in the meadows with her back to him, but now his mystery visitor was walking toward him with her lovely face in full view. As she approached, he stopped and called to her.

"Anne!"

"Frederick!" Anne answered pleased to see him. "You have come to meet me." But when she saw the look on his face, she knew something had changed. When he stopped walking, a fear gripped her heart.

"Anne Elliot!"

Upon hearing her maiden name, the name by which a young naval officer had known her, Anne knew her secret had been discovered.

"Yes, Frederick, I am Anne Elliot."

Husband and wife stared at each other from across a swath of meadow.

"Why did you not tell me?"

"I am so sorry, Frederick," Anne said with tears in her eyes. "Please forgive me."

In long strides, Frederick closed the distance between them. "Forgive you? It is I who is in need of forgiveness. I left you spewing unkind words and hateful epitaphs. I told you I would erase you from my memory, but the thing is, I never did. I have never stopped loving you, Anne," and he swept her up in his arms.

After having a good cry while in his embrace, Anne stepped away from Frederick and told him that this was the very topic she had wished to discuss with him, and she shared with him her reasons for keeping their former romance a secret.

"I was being selfish. I wanted you to fall in love with me as I am now. I am no longer a girl of nineteen years but a fully formed woman who needs you as much as flowers need the rain. I hope you understand, and I beg your forgiveness.

"You have had your say. Now I shall have mine. I want to be perfectly clear. There must be no cloud over our marriage. Anne Elliot, I offer myself to you again with a heart even more your own than when we parted eight years ago. I have loved none but you."

Anne collapsed in his arms and renewed her crying. After accepting his handkerchief and drying her tears, she asked why, if he had never stopped loving her, he had stayed away for eight years. "Why did you not come back?"

"I did come back—in '08. But because of your family's objections to our engagement, I could not call on you at Kellynch, and so I went to see Lady Russell. Although greatly surprised to see me in Somerset, she welcomed me into her home because she had good news to share. She told me you had received an offer of marriage from a prominent member of the local gentry, and she believed you would accept him."

"Yes, it is true that Charles Musgrove asked me to marry him, but I refused him. How could I marry anyone else when I was in love with you?"

"But you must understand I did not know of your refusal. I think it was about a year after my visit with Lady Russell that a new contingent of officers came aboard the *Laconia*, including an ensign by the name of Richard Musgrove. After learning he was from Somerset, I asked if he was related to Charles Musgrove, and he said they were brothers. After that, I questioned him about Charles's marriage, and he informed me that, yes, his brother had married Miss Elliot of Kellynch Hall."

"No! No! No!" Anne said, and she went to her knees, felled by the news that false reports had separated them for six years. Frederick knelt beside her, and with his big arms encircling her, he rocked her as if she were a child. "Six years! Six years have been lost!" Anne said, sobbing into his chest.

"Yes, six years have been lost," he said, taking her face in his big hands and wiping away her tears with his thumbs. "But that is but a fraction of the years we have ahead of us. Anne, we cannot change the past, but the future is firmly in our hands."

"But, Frederick, at some point in the future, when you have had time to think of all that has happened, will you be angry with me for not telling you of our past," Anne said in a moment of despair.

"Anne, you are blameless in all this. My pride, Lady Russell's interference, and your father's vanity all conspired against you, and because of our conceits, you lived in a lonely landscape with hardly a friend to

comfort you. It is *you* who should be angry with *me*."
After helping Anne up, Frederick pulled his wife into
an embrace and whispered, "From this point on, I
promise you calm seas and smooth sailing. I see no
dark clouds on the horizon."

Anne shook her head. "If we are to go forward in
complete harmony, then you must forgive yourself as
well, Frederick."

"Yes, I must learn to brook being happier than I
deserve, and by that I mean, being worthy of Anne
Elliott.

THE END

Other books by Mary Lydon Simonsen

From Sourcebooks:
Searching for Pemberley
The Perfect Bride for Mr. Darcy
A Wife for Mr. Darcy
Mr. Darcy's Bite

From Quail Creek Crossing:
Novels:
When they Fall in Love
Another Place in Time
Darcy on the Hudson
Becoming Elizabeth Darcy
Darcy Goes to War

Novellas:
For All the Wrong Reasons
Mr. Darcy's Angel of Mercy
A Walk in the Meadows at Rosings Park
Mr. Darcy Bites Back

Short Story:
Darcy and Elizabeth – Lost in Love
Darcy and Elizabeth – Behind Pemberley's Walls
Darcy and Elizabeth – Answered Prayers

Modern Novel:
The Second Date: Love Italian-American Style

Patrick Shea Mysteries:
Three's A Crowd
A Killing in Kensington
A Death in Hampden
Dying to Write
Murder by Moonlighting

Non-fiction:
The Mud Run Train Wreck –
A Disaster in the Irish-American Community

Printed in Great Britain
by Amazon

33419349R00088